T0162603

Imagine HISTORY

PERO KOVACESKI

WestBow
PRESS
A DIVISION OF THOMAS NELSON

WestBow Press books may be ordered through booksellers or by contacting:

WestBow Press
A Division of Thomas Nelson
1663 Liberty Drive
Bloomington, IN 47403
www.westbowpress.com
1-(866) 928-1240

ISBN: 978-1-4497-8195-8 (sc)
ISBN: 978-1-4497-8197-2 (hc)
ISBN: 978-1-4497-8196-5 (e)

Library of Congress Control Number: 2013900747

Printed in the United States of America

WestBow Press rev. date: 01/23/2014

PREFACE

Late one night in 2007, Pero was reading his Bible and a vision was given to him to write a book, this very book that you are holding.

In a moments time he received a 'download' of characters, chapters and even the title.

He had never had the intention of writing a book or becoming an author, yet God had other plans.

ACKNOWLEDGEMENTS

Firstly I would like to thank God for entrusting me with this precious book.

Thank you to my wife who has stood by me and believed in me every step of the way.

Thank you to my parents for my cherished upbringing and for giving me many opportunities through life.

Thank you to my younger brother for not just being a great brother but also a good friend.

I love all of you very much!

IN THE BEGINNING..

*S*imone, a somewhat naïve woman, thirty years of age with brown eyes and long black wavy hair, was walking to the New York City Library from her apartment. She carried three books in her arms which were to be returned.

As she walked along the quiet street, brown autumn leaves were falling around her from the trees that lined the road. In that tranquil moment, her mind escaped to an earlier memory of her life, where she experienced the same tranquility in a town called Ohrid. She was once more floating in a small wooden boat on the town's majestic lake.

She snapped out of her daze with a smile on her face as she realised she had arrived at the steps of the library. Walking inside, she returned the books and then stopped at the entry. As she stood there looking around and wondering where to search for her next good read she thought to herself, "Where should I go?"

Her eyes were drawn to a sign that read 'Non-Fiction' with an arrow on it pointing to the location.

"Non-fiction it is" she thought out aloud and headed towards that section.

When she arrived, she moved cautiously through the shelves full of books so as not to miss her next enthralling read. Arriving at the end of the aisle she proceeded around to the next one. There she noticed a white, hard cover leather book on the floor, halfway down the aisle. She walked over to it intending to put it back on the shelf. However, when she picked it up she examined its rough exterior running her fingers over it and noticed its many gold-edged pages. Flipping it over, the title caught her eye.. 'IMAGINE HISTORY', printed in bold, golden letters across its front and down the spine. Yet, when Simone examined the book further she noticed that it did not have a code like the rest of the books in the library. So as she concluded that it must belong to somebody she opened the front cover to see if there was any identification inside. What Simone saw shocked her. Written in the middle of the inside cover in Simone's own handwriting were the words..

'This
book belongs
to
Simone'.

She slapped the book shut in bewilderment, and whilst she examined it for the second time she said, "This is not my book."

With apprehension she once more opened the front cover and looked at the hand writing. She mumbled with exasperation "I didn't write this.."

Utterly confused, Simone walked over to the checkout counter and asked the lady behind the counter, "Hello Madame, could you please page a 'Simone' to come to the checkout? I'm sorry, I don't know her last name."

The lady smiled and said "Absolutely."

Simone thanked her and waited.

The intercom was in front of the lady so she held down the button that enabled the microphone and said in a gentle voice, "Please excuse this disturbance dear guests. If there is a 'Simone' in the library could you please come to the checkout counter. Thank you."

Simone thanked her again and the lady smiled and nodded, then continued with her duties.

Simone stepped back a few steps and waited patiently to see if the 'Simone' that owned the book, and who had the exact same style of handwriting as her would come.

A few minutes had passed and nobody claiming to be 'Simone' had showed up so she walked back to the counter and she spoke to the lady again, "Pardon me once more Madame.."

"Yes dear?" asked the lady.

"If 'Simone' shows up, would you mind giving her this note please?" Simone requested as she wrote down her own details and also that she had 'Simone's' book and wanted to give it back to her.

"Ok dear, will do" said the lady.

"Excellent. Thank you very much once more Madame" replied Simone.

They exchanged smiles and Simone walked out of the library with the book in hand. She headed home, her curiosity building, eager to see what this book was all about.

She reached her apartment building, John Tower, and proceeded to the elevator. When she got in she pressed the number '3' button, and the door closed. When it opened, she exited the elevator and fumbling around in her pocket for her keys she approached her apartment door, number '16'.

Simone entered her modest yet cosy apartment and headed straight for the lounge area where she placed the book on her coffee table. Wasting no time she sat on the rug by the table, next to the book.

She paused and stared at the book for a brief moment with contemplation. She then reached over to the book and opened the front cover to see the hand writing once more. She was amazed at the accuracy, the resemblance to her own hand writing was uncanny.

Tearing her eyes away from it, she glanced at the facing page and it was empty. So she turned the page and the book revealed its first chapter..

Chapter One

THE MACEDONIAN EMPIRE

4th Century BC.. King Philip II of Macedon and his son, Alexander, together with his mighty army had crossed the Macedonian border into Greece. They were heading for Chaeronea to battle against the Greeks.

*A*s Simone read these words she felt a gentle force emanating from the pages. Little did she know, the book itself was drawing her into the pages of history, and instantaneously Simone was taken to the time and place of what she was reading!

She was upright and at a standstill, looking headlong at the Greek army through a steel helmet that covered around her face. A wide, but relatively shallow river separated her from the Greek soldiers. She had a spear in her right hand and a shield emblazoned with the Vergina Sun in her left, her whole body weighed down by heavy armour.

"I must have fallen asleep" she reasoned. Although, continuing she thought, "But this can't be a dream. My senses are working perfectly, it's all so real.. What has happened to me?"

Then she became distracted from her train of thought by the clanking and rattling of steel, and so she turned her head to her right and noticed a soldier standing by her side. She turned her head even further and saw a multitude more soldiers, many of them on horses. She then quickly turned her head back to the front so that none of the men would notice her. It then became even clearer to her that she was in the front row of the Macedonian army!

Her mind began to race, she was very fearful and began to tremble. She asked herself, "How did I get here? Who brought me here?" She did not know what to do, but she did know that she wanted to go home, right then!

She turned her head to the left where she saw two men on horses standing in front of the army. It was King Philip and Alexander facing the Greeks. This all became too much for Simone, everything started to go black, and so she fainted.

Noticing a soldier fall to the ground, Alexander said to King Philip, "Excuse me Father," and yanked his horse, Bukefal's (Bucephelus) reins and rode towards where Simone was.

As he approached, he yelled out, "Soldier, are you alright?" There was no response at first and he moved closer.

Simone began to regain consciousness.

"Soldier!" shouted Alexander.

Her back was turned towards him. She slowly picked herself

up and then turned to face Alexander. When he saw Simone's face he became furious and yelled out, "Seize her!" to his soldiers.

Simone was terrified. The soldiers became puzzled: "Did he just say 'her'?" they thought.

The two soldiers that stood by her sides grabbed her by the arms and the soldier that stood behind her took her helmet off revealing Simone's horrified face as her long black hair tumbled down past her shoulders.

The soldiers gasped and began mumbling amongst themselves.

When King Philip saw Simone he was enraged and he rode his horse straight at her yelling, "How did the Greeks infiltrate my army?!"

He began breathing heavily in anger and turned towards his army and yelled at them further, demanding, "How did no man notice her?!" No soldier dared to speak at that moment.

Alexander, glaring at Simone yet addressing King Philip, asked, "Why would the Greeks send a woman?"

King Philip replied, "Because they are cowards and they love their men."

The soldiers that heard him say that laughed. The King looked at them and they fell silent once more. It was no laughing matter.

Alexander spoke to Simone saying, "You shall remain alive to see your people being slaughtered today, and when this battle is won I will slay you, assassin!"

Simone became even more terrified at Alexander's statement and she replied in disbelief, "Assassin? I am no assassin. I do not know how..."

"Silence!" shouted Alexander, and then he continued,

"How dare you speak! Not only that, how dare you speak lies!"

Simone began to cry and fell to her knees saying, "Please, there has been a mistake."

Alexander looked at the two soldiers that held her and said to them, "Get her on her feet, take her back beyond the army, where she will be able to watch her people die. And if she escapes, the both of you shall take her place!"

The two soldiers bowed their heads at Alexander, pulled Simone to her feet and took her to the far side past the army.

King Philip stated to Alexander, "We must prepare."

Alexander nodded his head and they rode back to the frontline.

Then King Philip said, "Where were we?.. Ah yes, as I was saying: I am glad to see that the Sacred Band of Thebes has also come to fight against us. We shall see how 'elite' they really are once we annihilate them" he laughed.

He then turned to Alexander and continued, "Alexander, you know what to do."

Alexander looked back at him and nodded his head in acknowledgment.

Across the river, the Greeks were becoming impatient watching the red and gold army opposite them.

An anxious Demosthenes yelled out from behind the Greek army, "What are these barbarians waiting for?!"

The Macedonians could see that the Greeks were becoming restless but they were not fazed.

The Greeks began hitting their shields with their swords

and spears in the hope that the Macedonians would become intimidated.

Instead, King Philip let out a raucous laugh, Alexander joined in and the Macedonian army followed. Their laughter was heard by the enemy, and it angered them deeply.

In response, a Greek General yelled out to his front infantry, commanding, "Charge!"

And so they charged at a walking pace in close formation towards the Macedonians.

King Philip could not believe what he was seeing, the Greeks making the first move! He was infuriated.

He turned to his army and yelled, "Let them come!"

Then he turned around to face the Greeks and yelled out to the leaders and Generals, "Stand before your pathetic army, you cowards!"

But of course they were too far to hear him.

King Philip looked at Alexander and said to him, "Call my Generals."

Alexander gestured to the Generals on either side of the army to approach, and they rode to the King and him. Behind them followed the other Generals who were positioned along the side of the army.

When they were all gathered King Philip addressed them, saying "As you can see, the battle plan has slightly changed. As they come towards us they will expose the Sacred Band behind them. Alexander, you will take our left infantry and go around their front infantry and attack the Sacred Band. Our right infantry will follow and I will attack their frontline head on with our frontline. Understood?!"

Alexander and the Generals nodded their heads in agreement

and rode off to their respective positions, with Alexander in front of his left infantry.

King Philip looked at his frontline and called out, "Maintain the phalanxes whilst the enemy approaches, and on my command you will attack!"

Now, as the Greeks got close to the Macedonians the gap was wide enough for Alexander to launch his attack. He reached back with his right hand, grabbed his sword and pointed it at the Greeks yelling with a mighty voice, "FOR THE GLORY OF MACEDONIA.. CHARGE!"

Bukefal (Bucephalus) launched Alexander towards the enemy, and his screaming left infantry followed.

The foot soldiers moved with such speed and force in formation that they almost kept up with the horses charging in front of them. They quickly crossed the shallow river and they passed around the advancing Greek infantry.

Stunned by this, the advancing Greeks did not know what to do, were they to return or keep advancing? So, they stopped and awaited orders.

Behind them, the frustrated Greek Generals were yelling and making abrupt hand gestures at them to keep them advancing, so they continued on.

Meanwhile, the Greek Generals in charge of their right infantry commanded, "Charge at Alexander now!" and the right infantry charged towards him.

Then the leader of the Sacred Band cried out with rage, "Kill those Macedonian scum!" and they charged also.

Alexander had broken through the gap and he clashed with

the Sacred Band, whilst part of his left infantry clashed with the Greeks' right infantry.

The General of the Macedonian right infantry yelled out, "Charge their left infantry now!" and so they did.

Simone watched on in horror as men on both sides were being slaughtered. She tried to look away but a soldier grabbed her head and threatened, "Watch or I will take your eyes out."

Confusion abounded amongst the Greeks at Alexander's bold move. He was being surrounded by the Greeks, but then the Macedonian right infantry arrived and unleashed havoc upon them.

King Philip and his men watched the killing frenzy that Alexander and his men were engaged in, wanting desperately to be involved in it.

When the King saw that the advancing Greeks had reached the river's edge he unsheathed his sword and yelled out, "Annihilate them!"

His soldiers charged, yelling and screaming like mad men. King Philip was leading the charge.

They clashed in the middle of the river, blood from the dead and wounded flowed downstream turning it red.

The vicious battle was too much for some Greeks and so they threw down their weapons and shields fleeing for their lives.

Demosthenes was amongst the retreating group.

When King Philip saw that he and his men were the victors

of the clash at the river, they charged towards the main battle at full speed.

The remaining Greeks realised that the Macedonians had the upper hand and so when they saw King Philip charging towards them they threw down their weapons and shields and raised their arms into the air in surrender before the King had even reached them to join the battle. The Macedonians ceased fighting the moment the Greeks had unarmed themselves.

They raised their swords and spears into the air shouting a victorious roar.

As King Philip arrived, all of the remaining Greeks bowed down on their knees to the Macedonian King.

All of the Macedonian army once more lifted their weapons into the air whilst shouting repeatedly,

"Hail King Philip and Alexander of Macedon!"

The Greeks rose to their feet and were forced to join in, and they did so, although reluctantly.

King Philip and Alexander grabbed each other by the forearms shaking hands and then they embraced. The King lifted his hand and then everyone fell silent. Then he exclaimed to the crowd, "Today, a Macedonian King has become ruler over Greece!"

The Macedonians' cheers were deafening.

Alexander said to King Philip, "Father, the Macedonian Sun shines brightly over Greece today."

King Philip laughed and replied, "Indeed it does my son, indeed it does."

Then a Greek General approached King Philip and bowed on his knee and said, "Great King, may I speak?"

Philip answered saying, "Speak."

"Great King," said the General, "May we bury our dead?"

The King scoffed at the General and yelled his answer at him, "That is your question?!" He paused, then continued with much derision, "That is the least of your troubles now Greek! And No! You may not bury them, they shall lay there and rot!" he growled through gritted teeth.

The General bowed his head in sorrow.

Then Philip turned to Alexander and said, "Now that we have secured Greece we can focus on Persia."

Alexander smiled and nodded with acknowledgment.

Then, Alexander remembered Simone and yelled out, "Bring me the assassin!"

The two soldiers who were guarding Simone had brought her from across the river once the battles had ceased. Immediately upon hearing Alexander's command they brought Simone before him, throwing her to the ground.

Alexander climbed off of his horse and walked over to her saying, "Remember what I said to you assassin?"

Simone did not answer him. She did not dare to look up at him. She began to tremble with the fear of dying.

Alexander spoke sternly, "Look at me assassin!"

Simone slowly turned her head to look up at him. But all of a sudden, there Alexander stood with his sword raised, and he struck Simone down!

Everything went black in an instant and then she found herself back on the floor of her apartment next to the book on the table. She screamed in terror and frantically checked herself for any signs of blood or trauma. But she did not find any blood; neither did she find any lacerations or wounds of any kind. Not even a scar!

Terrified, yet relieved, she sat up breathless and stared at the book with a mixture of emotions and thoughts.

As she calmed down and her heavy breathing eased, she exclaimed out aloud, "What just happened to me?"

She paused, then thought, "I just witnessed history.."

She paused once more. She looked at the book for a moment. Her first thought was to close the book and destroy it, but knowing that she was brought back home safe and alive, she questioned herself, "What if I turn the page over?"

A moment passed. Her curiosity got the better of her, so she turned the page over and revealed the next chapter..

Chapter Two

THE ROMAN EMPIRE

1st Century BC.. Up until his time, Julius Caesar had done more for Rome than any of his predecessors. He had expanded the empire with much bloodshed. He left Rome many times and spent years at war and almost always came back victorious.

He was an immoral fornicator, even cavorting with married women and Queens of foreign lands. The most famous of which was Cleopatra, who bore him a child after he had made her Queen of Egypt.

Once more, Simone was taken to the time and place of what she was reading.

She was lying on what appeared to be an antique lounge. She sat up abruptly and looked around. Looking at the layout of the large, opulent room she realised she was in some sort of palace.

She then heard a voice calling out repeatedly, "Julia!.. Julia!"

After a moment, the person calling out the name walked into the room. Simone stood up but was also speechless. It was Julius Caesar!

She recognised him from the portraits and busts she had seen of him in books she had read and museums she had visited.

Caesar looked at Simone and said, "There you are Sister. Why did you not answer me when I called out to you?"

Simone was shocked at what Caesar had said to her. He had referred to her as his sister, Julia.

She realised that she had to answer his question, and so she said, "Forgive me Brother, I was asleep."

Caesar smiled and said, "I wanted to inform you that I shall be leaving to attend the meeting, and will not be back until late."

Simone replied, "Be safe Brother."

Caesar smiled at her and left the room.

Simone laughed as she sat down saying out aloud, "How can this be? This is unbelievable!" And then as it occurred to her, her expression changed and she panicked, "Oh no!..How am I going to get back home? I don't want to be killed.. Again! And if that were to happen would it even work again?"

She was now a bit frantic, "What have I done?"

After a moment of worrying had passed she reasoned, "I am going to have to accept this for now and try to find a way to return home."

She stood up and walked over to the nearest window. Her

breath was taken away by the view of Rome in all of its glory. Then her gaze was interrupted by the whistling of a kingbird that flew over the window she was at and down into the courtyard below.

Simone smiled, but then a flock of crows surrounded the kingbird and tore it to pieces. Simone became sad and walked away from the window, but then stopped in her tracks.

She exclaimed out aloud, "That is one of the prophesies of Caesar's assassination!"

She stormed out of the room yelling out repeatedly, "Julius!.. Julius!"

Simone could not find him but Caesar heard her cries and called out to her saying, "Over here Julia!"

Simone followed his voice and when she saw him she embraced him.

He saw the distress on her face and asked her, "What is wrong Julia?"

Simone answered, "Please Julius, do not go to the meeting."

Caesar became puzzled, "Why not?"

Simone replied, "Death awaits you."

Caesar grabbed Simone by the arms, "Enough!" he yelled. Then continued, "I do not know what you and Calpurnia are up to, but that is no laughing matter."

Then Simone remembered from her studies that Calpurnia was Caesar's wife and so she said to him, "Brother, I tell you the truth, neither have I seen Calpurnia, nor are we up to anything."

Now, Caesar became distressed and he pondered, "This is very strange, Calpurnia told me of her dream that I was lying in her arms, lifeless, with blood flowing out of my body. And now, you tell me that death awaits me at the meeting."

There was a pause, "How do you know? What did you see?"

Simone answered, "A kingbird was torn to pieces by a flock of crows."

"That is very eerie" replied Caesar with a distressed look. "In that case, I will postpone the meeting until a later date and that way I will avoid death. The gods must favour me for giving signs to both of you."

Satisfied with his decision, he smiled at Simone and departed.

Simone returned to her room and lied on the lounge and thought with disbelief, "Why did I try to prevent a dictator from being dethroned?"

Simone did not realise it, but she had been endowed with the love of a sister towards a brother.

Meanwhile, Marcus Antonius arrived, Caesar's Military Commander, Administrator and one time enemy. He approached Caesar and said to him, "Hail Caesar."

Caesar nodded and Antonius continued, "Your escort is ready to take you to the meeting."

Caesar replied, "Antonius, postpone the meeting until another day."

Antonius did not ask why but said, "Yes Caesar" and walked off to inform the waiting Senators.

On his way out, Antonius was met by Decimus Albinus, Caesar's distant cousin and a General.

Albinus called out, "Greeting Antonius. Are you not meant to be escorting Caesar?"

Antonius did not stop, yet answered him, "Greetings

Albinus, no, I will not be escorting Caesar. He is postponing the meeting until another day."

Albinus did not say another word but rushed to Caesar and when he approached him he said, "Hail Caesar."

Caesar nodded his head as Albinus asked, "Caesar, may I ask you a question?"

Caesar nodded once more and Albinus continued, "Why has the meeting been postponed?"

Caesar replied, "My dear Albinus, both Calpurnia and Julia have warned me of danger on separate occasions in regards to today's meeting. Calpurnia with a dream and Julia with a vision. I am taking it as a forewarning, I do not want to be taking any risks."

Albinus was shocked and replied, "Caesar, can you imagine the reaction of the Senators when word reaches them that the great 'Caesar' is afraid to leave the palace because he is worried by women's dreams and visions? Worse yet, what will the people of Rome and beyond say and think of you?"

Caesar considered this for a moment and replied, "You are right Albinus. I can not appear to be weak. My rule will be questioned."

Albinus smiled and said, "Wise decision Caesar." Then he yelled out, "Messenger!"

Immediately a messenger approached them and Albinus said to him, "Marcus Antonius is going to postpone the meeting, leave now and tell him that the meeting will go ahead as planned. Hurry!"

The messenger nodded his head and ran off.

Albinus turned to Caesar and said, "Shall we?" pointing to the exit.

Caesar replied, "Yes."

And so they departed. Outside were Caesar's soldiers, and a crowd had gathered at the outer court with people anxious to catch a glimpse of Caesar. When he stepped outside, the crowds cheered. He smiled and lifted his hand up at them.

When he and Albinus arrived at the bottom of the palatial steps the soldiers surrounded them and made way for them through the crowds. The people followed them.

One man tried to approach Caesar but was stopped by a soldier who demanded, "What do you want?!"

The man replied, "Please.. I must give this to Caesar" showing the soldier a sealed scroll.

The soldier saw the urgency and distress on the man's face and said, "I will give the scroll to him." And so he took it from him.

The man said, "Please, it is of the utmost importance, time is of the essence!"

The soldier did not acknowledge this, but kept walking.

The man stopped and the crowd of people pushed past him as he watched Caesar walking away.

Caesar and Albinus saw Antonius approaching them. He greeted them, "Hail Caesar" then continued as he walked with them, "Why the sudden change Caesar?"

Caesar smiled and put his hand on Albinus' shoulder, who was standing on his left side, and answered, "Dear Albinus opened my eyes and convinced me."

After a short while they arrived at the steps of the meeting hall where they were met by a few Senators and a scholar carrying a pile of scrolled petitions that were to be opened and discussed at the meeting.

The soldier carrying the scroll from the man in the crowd approached the scholar and handed it over to him, saying, "For Caesar."

The scholar nodded and the soldier walked back to his position.

Caesar, Antonius, Albinus, the Senators and the scholar ascended the steps of the hall. Soldiers and civilians were not permitted past the first step.

About halfway up Albinus said, "Antonius, I must speak with you urgently."

They all stopped and Caesar and Antonius looked at Albinus in bewilderment.

Then Antonius angrily replied, "What could be so important that it could not wait until the end of the meeting? That you would embarrass yourself and myself before Caesar!"

They all stared at Albinus but he did not reply.

Antonius looked at Caesar and said to him, "Please excuse us Caesar, we will not be long."

Caesar nodded, stared at Albinus momentarily then continued up the stairs.

As Antonius and Albinus stood on the steps, Antonius, still angry, demanded, "Why did you do that? What do you want?"

Now, right before Caesar and the Senators entered the hall they stopped so that the scholar would hand over the petitions. Once he did that, Caesar and the Senators entered the hall and the scholar departed from there for he was not permitted to enter. He walked down the steps diagonally so as not to intrude on Antonius and Albinus' privacy.

Once Caesar entered the hall, the waiting Senators rose to

their feet with applause. Caesar smiled again and sat in his seat, the Senators also took their seats.

The Senator that was carrying the petitions put them on the table beside Caesar, and then took his seat.

Caesar remembered the words Calpurnia and Julia had spoken to him and began to be troubled by them. He became agitated and restless. Wasting no time and wanting to get through the meeting as fast as possible he announced, "Let us begin, the meeting is now in session. Before we read the petitions is there anything on the agenda that we need to discuss?"

Caesar looked around at the Senators. One of them stood up and said, "Caesar, will you grant my brother a pardon to return home?"

Caesar dismissively replied, "Do not waste mine or the Senators' time with such requests. Your brother deserved death, I showed mercy in exiling him."

Now other Senators stood up and voiced their objections against Caesar's ruling and they became very disruptive, although this was not out of the ordinary at a meeting of this kind.

The Senator that asked for the clemency began walking towards Caesar and yelled, "Will you pardon my brother?!"

Caesar stood up and yelled out, "Silence!"

The Senators became quiet. He looked around at them and said, "I see now that many of you object to my decision, and for that reason we shall discuss this matter, but at a later time. Now take your seats."

Caesar sat back down and as he did so the Senator that had approached him pinned down his hands on the armrests. Caesar was stunned and said, "What is the meaning of this?!"

The Senator whispered, "This is the signal."

As he said that, another Senator rushed out of his seat and with a dagger he attacked Caesar, striking him on the side of his neck.

The attacker, overcome by nerves, ran back not realising he had only grazed Caesar's skin.

Caesar then headbutted the Senator who was holding him down, knocking him out and he fell on the floor.

The attacker that had struck Caesar saw that he had not been successful and so gathering his nerves, charged at him once more.

Caesar quickly reached for his stylus on the table and when the attacker got close enough he lodged it in his eye, before the attacker could strike him. The fatally wounded attacker collapsed on top of the unconscious Senator.

The others were already on edge but now they became anxious as well. Caesar looked at them and yelled, "Who is behind this treachery?!"

Then the Senators produced daggers and charged at him. Caesar was overcome by shock and froze. He knew that calling out for help would be futile. He braced himself and when the Senators reached him they slashed and stabbed him repeatedly from all sides. Some also wounding themselves and each other in the frenzy.

Caesar collapsed, and his body lay lifeless on the floor. The Senators stood over him in shock. Their white clothes were covered with Caesar's blood.

Then one of them, Marcus Brutus, a main conspirator and a close friend of Julius, tried to speak to the Senators but they all fled.

Brutus looked at Caesar's lifeless body for a moment and then he too ran off joining the others.

Antonius and Albinus were still engaged in conversation on the steps. All of a sudden, they were interrupted by the screams of the Senators flooding out of the hall and down the stairs.

The crowds were puzzled.

Antonius turned to the soldiers and yelled out to them, "Stay in formation and do not let the people break through."

He then turned around and ran up the steps into the hall.

Albinus smiled, his task of stalling Antonius was accomplished, and he headed off down the stairs.

Now, by this point the hall was empty and when Antonius arrived at the meeting place he froze with shock upon seeing Caesar lying on the floor in a pool of blood.

Antonius ran to him and fell on his knees next to Caesar but did not touch him, there was nothing he could do but look on in horror.

After a moment, he stood up and ran outside to the edge of the steps and screamed, "Caesar is dead!"

When the crowds heard what he had said they began to wail.

Many more people gathered because of the commotion.

Generals and dignitaries ran up the steps wanting to see Caesar.

When they gathered around Caesar's body, they looked on in shock and disbelief.

As word quickly spread through Rome, panic ensued.

Simone, still lying on the lounge, heard people running around and screaming outside. She jumped up and ran over to the window seeing absolute pandemonium.

A servant girl walked up to the entry of Simone's room, Simone turned around and permitted her, "Enter."

The girl entered as Simone continued, "What day is it?"

The girl replied, "Why it is the Ides of March, your highness."

Simone remembered from her studies back at school that Caesar was assassinated on the 'Ides of March'. Then she said to the girl, "Did you come to tell me that Julius is dead?"

The girl bowed her head in sadness and cried, answering, "Yes, your highness."

Simone also knew what was about to unfold in Rome and beyond. Knowing that she was 'Julia', Caesar's sister, she had a son and had to warn him of what had happened. So she said to the girl, "Quickly, summon me a messenger."

The servant girl ran out of the room to fetch what Simone asked for. Within a minute or so, a messenger appeared at the door and Simone told him to enter, "Write down what I am about to tell you."

As the messenger prepared himself at the desk with a scroll in front of him, Simone walked back over to the window and the messenger said, "Ready, your highness."

Simone spoke, "Octavian, my son, your adoptive father, Julius Caesar, has been assassinated. I have not made a mistake, I did say 'Father' because he adopted you from me not long ago. This means that you are the next Caesar! Yet as you know, Antonius is consul and is popular with the soldiers and he will proclaim himself as Caesar's political heir. Your young age and inexperience in politics and war are your disadvantages, although that is why you are there at the military school in Apollonia."

She continued, "Yet, you must leave at once and become a

private citizen to avoid detection and somehow return home to Rome because your life is in danger, all of Julius' family are in danger. In the end, however, you will claim what is rightfully yours. You will be the first and greatest Emperor that Rome will ever see. You will be known as 'Augustus'!"

She walked over to the messenger, and taking the stylus, signed *'Julia'*.

Then, she instructed the messenger, "Now, seal the scroll and deliver it to my son at once."

The messenger nodded and ran out of the room as Simone returned to the window.

Back at the meeting hall, Antonius and the Generals decided to carry Caesar's body down to his people. As they walked down the steps with the body, the people saw it covered in blood and they erupted in anger, crying out, "Murder!" and "Avenge Caesar!" repeatedly.

The guilty Senators fled Rome only to return once the matter had calmed down. The conspiracy however, was far from over.

The people dragged benches, tables and other materials from any place they could find and piled them on top of one another. They shouted for an immediate cremation as they could not bear to see Caesar in such a way.

Antonius and the Generals complied, and they placed Caesar's body on top of the pyre and then set it alight.

Then, a full scale riot erupted, the soldiers could not control the multitude. Some people remembered seeing the Senators running out of the hall with blood all over them, and so they made their own judgments that they were the assassins. Infuriated by this, they picked up burning pieces of wood from the pyre and ran to the houses of the Senators to set them on fire, hoping the Senators would be inside.

Back at the palace, Simone was still staring out of the window, when she heard screams from within the palace. She did not move.

Then, a hooded man entered her room.

She became aware that someone was there, but did not turn around because she knew why that person was there. Simone closed her eyes.

The man revealed a blood stained dagger, then raised it and plunged it into Simone's back.

It ended Julia's life, but it sent Simone home.

When she returned, the force once more threw her down, yet this time she calmly felt around her back, making sure that she was not hurt.

As she suspected, there was nothing. She smiled with anticipation, then quickly crawled to the book and was excited to experience the next chapter.

As she turned the page over, she wondered what the next chapter might hold.

Chapter Three

THE MESSIAH

The Jewish people were waiting for their promised Messiah, their Redeemer, and not just theirs but all of humanity's. There was talk of a Prophet who was among them who some thought could be the One. Little did most people know that He *was* the One. God was with them in human form!

As Simone read this, she was taken to this time and place in history.

She found herself on a seashore facing the water and lying in a curled up position. She was wearing black robes. She was in pain, suffering many things. She groaned and cried from the overwhelming agony. A slow and steady flow of blood dripped out of her ears and nose as she lay there.

She asked aloud, "What is happening?"

She paused, then groaned, "I don't want this, I want to go home."

The pain increased when she spoke, so she whispered, "God.. Help me."

She closed her eyes and all of a sudden, she heard a voice and quickly opened her eyes as the voice said, "Come to Me all you who labour and are heavy laden, and I will give you rest. Take My yoke upon you and learn from Me, for I am gentle and lowly in heart, and you will find rest for your souls. For My yoke is easy and My burden is light."

The voice echoed in her mind and body. Her spirit within was lifted, her strength renewed enough for her to turn around and see who was speaking to her, yet there was nobody next to her.

She saw a great gathering of about five thousand people on the foot of the mount not far from where she was, yet it could not have been one of those people, because the voice she heard was of someone speaking next to her.

Simone knew that she did not imagine the voice, and recollected that she had called out to God right before she heard it.

Puzzled, she asked, "God?"

A moment passed, and nothing. She sighed and felt foolish, grumbling, "What am I doing?"

Suddenly, she was interrupted by the same voice, saying, "I am the way, the truth and the life. No one comes to the Father except through Me."

Simone was shocked, her eyes opened wide and her breathing became labored as she came to the realisation of Whose words she was hearing, and that He could be the One talking to her.

The One that she was told about whenever she walked past a church or whenever she was stopped on a street corner back home. Confused, she said, "No, no. This cannot be true."

The voice continued, "I am the resurrection and the life. They who believe in Me, though they may die, will live."

Simone began to weep as emotional pain swept through her body.

Being a Jew herself, she said, "What have *we* done?"

The voice continued, "Thus it was written, and thus it is necessary for the Christ to suffer and to rise from the dead the third day."

That brought some comfort to her, yet she did not understand why 'the Christ' had to die.

She sat up, barely able to lift herself, and once more looked towards the multitude.

Simone gasped, losing her breath for a moment, and then said, "Jesus." She could not believe that she was actually looking at Him.

Her eyes would not look away. Jesus was returning her gaze as He walked amongst the people speaking to them the same words Simone was hearing in the distance.

"How is He doing that?" she thought, because He did not yell when He spoke.

Once more, she heard His voice, "With people this is impossible, but with God all things are possible, and the things which are impossible with people are possible with God."

Jesus was answering all of her questions and yet, He spoke with relevance to what He was saying to the people.

Simone lost sight of Jesus in the crowd, then a jolt of pain gripped her body making her fall back down and she curled herself up on the ground.

Simone thought, "I cannot bear this pain any longer, I had to die in the previous chapters to go home."

She looked at the sea, then slowly and painfully began to roll herself towards it. The moment she felt the water touch her, she heard Jesus' voice, "Simone."

She stopped, as Jesus continued, "Simone, you just heard Me say 'Come to Me. I am the way, the truth and the life' and yet you still went in the opposite direction which leads to death and an eternity of torment and suffering apart from Me. Therefore, I say to you that you would have died in your sins because you did not, and still do not, believe that I am He, the Son of God."

Simone began to cry and called out to Him, saying "Jesus! I believe!" she paused then continued, "I know now that You are the Messiah."

Jesus replied, "Simone, you have passed from death into life."

She felt overjoyed by the whole experience, yet she still felt immense pain all over her body.

Then, all of a sudden, she had a revelation, "Jesus is a healer" she said out aloud.

She remembered this because of all the people that had spoken to her about Him, preaching the Gospel and spreading the Word.

Then she thought, "I must go to Him, if I only touch a piece of His garment, I will be made well."

Simone picked herself up very slowly and managed to stand on her feet, and she made her way to Jesus at a weak, slow and unsteady pace.

She heard His voice once more, "My grace is sufficient for you, My strength is made perfect in weakness. God loves you Simone, He loves the world, that is why He gave Me to it, His only begotten Son, that whoever believes in Me should not perish but have everlasting life. I have come as a light into the world, that whoever believes in Me should not abide in darkness."

He continued, "I did not come to condemn the world but to *save* the world. They who believe in Me are not condemned; but they who do not believe are condemned already, the words that I have spoken will judge them in the last day. For I have not spoken on My own authority; but God the Father who sent Me gave Me a command, what I should say and what I should speak. And I know that His command is everlasting life. And this is eternal life, that people may know Him, the only true God, and I, Jesus Christ His Son, whom He has sent. Those who believe in Me have everlasting life, and those who do not believe in Me shall not see life, but the wrath of God abides on them. I and the Father are one, I give you eternal life and you shall never perish."

Simone had never heard such great promises. This made her more determined to reach Jesus.

Jesus continued to walk through the crowds and preach to them, saying "Blessed are the meek, for they shall inherit the earth. Blessed are the merciful, for they shall obtain mercy. Blessed are the pure in heart, for they shall see God. Blessed are the peacemakers, for they shall be called children of God. Blessed are those who are persecuted for righteousness sake, for theirs is the kingdom of heaven. Blessed are those who have not seen and yet believe. Blessed are those who hear the Word of God and keep it!"

Simone reached the edge of the crowd. As she continued

through the crowd she was bumping into the people, her pain intensified and she fell on her hands and knees.

Full of determination, she began to crawl.

The people that noticed her moved away from her, as she was regarded as an 'unclean' person because she was very ill.

Some yelled abuse at her, telling her to go to the crowd where all the sick people were gathered, away from everyone else. Yet, others looked and felt pity for her.

Simone ignored them all and pressed on.

In the crowd was a mixture of young and old, rich and poor, scribes, Pharisees and Sadducees, Roman soldiers, Generals, and Jesus' twelve Apostles.

The only reason why the scribes, Pharisees, Sadducees, soldiers and Generals were there was to arrest Jesus if He spoke out against any of them. Little did they know that there were people in their ranks that followed Jesus. Some were present in the crowds, wearing civilian clothing.

Jesus continued to speak, saying, "Ask, and it will be given to you, seek, and you will find, knock, and it will be opened to you."

Then, a man yelled out from the crowd, "Teach us how to pray!"

Jesus smiled and replied, speaking to all, "When you pray, say: Our Father in heaven, Hallowed be Your name. Your kingdom come. Your will be done on earth as it is in heaven. Give us day by day our daily bread. And forgive us our sins, as we also forgive those who sin against us. And lead us not into temptation but deliver us from evil. For Yours is the kingdom, and the power and the glory, forever. Amen."

Jesus paused, then continued, "Whatever you ask God in My name He will give you. Whatever things you ask in

My name when you pray, believe that you receive them, and you will have them. And whenever you pray, if you have anything against anyone, forgive them, that God may also forgive you your trespasses. But if you do not forgive neither will God forgive you. Forgive people from your heart. Take heed to yourselves. If anyone sins against you, rebuke them, and if they repent, forgive them. And if they sin seven times in a day, and seven times in a day they return to you, saying, 'I repent', you shall forgive them. God desires mercy and not sacrifice."

He continued, "I say to you, love your enemies, bless those who curse you, do good to those who hate you, and pray for those who spitefully use you and persecute you. And just as you want others to do to you, you do to them likewise. Do good, give, hoping for nothing in return, and those who want to borrow from you do not turn away."

"Be merciful," He said, "just as God is merciful. Do not judge, and you shall not be judged. For with what judgment you judge, you will be judged; and with the measure you use, it will be measured back to you. Do not condemn, and you will not be condemned, yet I say to you for every idle word people may speak, they will give an account of it in the day of judgment. For, by your words you will be justified, and by your words you will be condemned. What comes out of a person, that defiles a person. For from within, out of the heart of a person, proceed evil thoughts, adulteries, fornications, murders, thefts, covetousness, wickedness, deceit, lewdness, an evil eye, blasphemy, pride, foolishness. All these things come from within and defile a person."

"For nothing is secret that will not be revealed, nor anything hidden that will not be known and come to light."

Simone stopped crawling to rest for a moment and saw that she was closing in on Jesus, because as He spoke He sometimes stood still for a moment.

Simone began crawling again as Jesus continued speaking, saying, "Enter through the narrow gate; for wide is the gate and broad is the way that leads to destruction, and there are many who go in by it. Not everyone who says to Me, 'Lord, Lord' shall enter the kingdom of heaven, but they who do the will of God shall enter. For what will it profit a person if they gain the whole world yet lose their own soul?"

"Watch and pray, so that you do not enter into temptation. The spirit is indeed willing, but the flesh is weak. It is impossible that no offences should come, but woe to those through whom they do come! Woe to the world because of offences!"

He continued, "In the world you will have tribulation; but be of good cheer; I have overcome the world. Remember that it hated Me before it hated you, because I testify of it that its works are evil. Every kingdom divided against itself is brought to desolation, and every city or house divided against itself shall not stand."

"The light of the body is the eye. If therefore your eye is good your whole body will be full of light. But if your eye is evil, your whole body will be full of darkness."

"Take heed, and beware of covetousness, for a person's life does not consist of the abundance of the things they possess."

Jesus paused, then said, "These things I have spoken to you, that you should not be made to stumble, that in Me you may have peace. But I say to you REPENT! For the kingdom of heaven is at hand. There will be more joy in the presence of the angels of God in heaven over one sinner who repents than over ninety nine righteous persons who need no repentance."

Finally, Simone reached Jesus and whilst looking at the ground she reached out behind Him and touched the hem of His garment.

Immediately, she felt in her body that she was healed of her affliction and with a heavy sigh of relief she stood up from her hands and knees and looked at Jesus.

And Jesus, knowing in Himself that power had perceived out of Him, turned around slowly and looked at Simone.

He smiled and said to her, "Daughter, be of good cheer; your faith has made you well."

Simone stood there speechless, with tears of joy, gazing at Jesus.

When the people witnessed the miracle they praised and worshipped God.

Simone remained with her eyes and ears affixed on Jesus.

Jesus smiled and said to the people, "Yes! Praise and worship God!"

He continued to walk amongst them saying, "But the hour is coming, and now is, when the true worshippers will worship God the Father in spirit and in truth; for God is seeking such to worship Him. God is Spirit, and those who worship Him must worship Him in spirit and truth."

Jesus then said, "And how much more will your heavenly Father give the Holy Spirit to those who ask Him."

Then, Jesus looked up into the heavens and said, "Sanctify them by Your truth, Your word is truth."

Jesus looked back at the crowds and said, "For this cause I have come into the world, that I should bear witness to the truth. Everyone who is of the truth hears My voice. And you shall know the truth, and the truth shall make you free. For the law was given through Moses but grace and truth come through Me. And whoever is ashamed of Me and My words in this adulterous and sinful generation, of them I will be ashamed when I arrive in the glory of My Father with the holy angels. Whoever confesses Me before people, I will confess that person before My Father. But whoever denies Me before people, I will deny them before My Father."

"Blessed are they who are not offended because of Me. I am the bread of life. I am the living bread which came down from heaven. The bread that I shall give is My flesh, which I shall give for the life of the world. For this is My blood of the new covenant, which is shed for many for the remission of sins."

He continued, "I have come that you may have life, and that you may have it more abundantly. I am the good shepherd. The good shepherd gives his life for his sheep."

"All that the Father gives Me will come to Me, and the one who comes to Me I will by no means cast out. For I have come down from heaven, not to do My own will, but the will of Him who sent Me. I did not come to be served, but to serve, and to give My life as a ransom for many. If anyone serves Me, let them follow Me, and where I am, there My servants will be also. If anyone serves Me, them My Father will honour."

Jesus stopped for a moment, and then spoke again, "They who are faithful in what is least are faithful also in much; and they who are unjust in what is least are unjust also in much. And if you have not been faithful in what is another persons, who will give you what is your own? No servant can serve two masters; for either they will hate the one and love the other, or else they will be loyal to the one and despise the other. You cannot serve God and Mammon."

"I have not come to call the righteous, but sinners, to repentance. I have come to save that which was lost."

Jesus pointed to a group of children that were present and said, "It is not the will of God that one of these little ones should perish. Therefore I say to you, do not worry about your life, what you will eat or what you will drink; nor about your body, what you will put on. Is not life more than food and the body more than clothing? Look at the birds of the air for they neither sow nor reap nor gather into barns; yet your heavenly Father feeds them. Are you not of more value than they? Which of you by worrying can add one cubit to your stature? Therefore, do not worry saying, 'What shall we eat?' or 'What shall we drink?' or 'What shall we wear?'. For your heavenly Father knows that you need all these things. But seek first the kingdom of God and His righteousness, and all these things shall be added to you. The kingdom of God is within you! Have faith in God!"

Then a man called out to Jesus, asking, "Teacher, which is the great commandment in the Law?"

Jesus said to him, "'You shall love the Lord your God with all your heart, with all your soul, and with all your mind'. This is the first and great commandment. And the second is like it: 'You shall love your neighbour as yourself.' On these two commandments hang all the Law and the Prophets. Yet, a new commandment I give to you, that you love one another, as I have loved you. Whoever breaks one of these commandments, and teaches people to do the same, shall be called least in the kingdom of heaven; but whoever does and teaches them, they shall be called great in the kingdom of heaven. They who have My commandments and keep them, it is they who love Me. And they that love Me shall be loved by My Father, and I will love them and manifest Myself to them. My Father and I will come to them and make Our home with them."

"God will also give you another Helper, that He may abide in you forever, the Spirit of truth, the Holy Spirit. For God does not give the Spirit by measure. Every sin and blasphemy will be forgiven people, but the blasphemy against the Holy Spirit will not be forgiven. Whoever speaks against the Holy Spirit, will *not* be forgiven. They will be subject to eternal condemnation."

"The Spirit of the Lord is upon Me. Because He has anointed Me to preach the Gospel to the poor, another reason I have come. He has sent Me to heal the broken hearted, to proclaim liberty to the captives and recovery of sight to the blind, to set at liberty those who are oppressed."

Jesus looked at where all the 'sick' people were gathered, and walked towards them.

The multitude noticed what Jesus was doing, so they who were seated stood up and everyone, including Simone, walked with Jesus.

Simone was confused and wondered what was going on.

The 'sick' saw that Jesus was walking towards them and so they began to call out to Him, pleading and begging, "Jesus! Have mercy on us!"

There were three blind men present and when they heard the people calling out they too joined in. The multitude made a circle around the 'sick', yet kept their distance.

As Jesus reached them, those who were ill became silent. Then a blind man by the name of Bartimaeus knew that Jesus had arrived and called out to Him, saying, "Son of God, have mercy on me!"

Jesus looked at him and knew that Bartimaeus was blind yet still He asked him, "What do you want Me to do for you?" Jesus wanted Bartimaeus to ask for what he needed.

He answered, "Lord, that I may receive my sight."

Jesus smiled and said, "Receive your sight."

Immediately, he received his sight and Jesus said to him, "Your faith has made you well."

Bartimaeus began to squint because he had never seen sunlight, he praised God and all of the people that had seen the miracle did so too.

Jesus saw the remaining two blind men that stood behind Bartimaeus and asked them, "Do you believe that I am able to do this?"

Although the men could not see Jesus, they knew in their hearts that He was speaking to them. They both answered, "Yes, Lord."

Jesus put His hands over their eyes and said, "According to your faith let it be to you."

And their eyes were opened. The blind men received their sight. With tears in their eyes, one shouted, "Praise God Almighty!" and the other, "Glory be to God Most High!"

The crowds cheered.

A leper walked over to Jesus and said, "Lord, if You are willing, You can make me clean of this leprosy."

Then, Jesus reached out His hand and put it on the man's shoulder and said, "I am willing; be clean."

Immediately, the man was cleansed of his leprosy, and his

skin was restored to its original form. He was so overjoyed that he fell on his knees and cried.

The crowds marveled and glorified God once they had seen the miracle.

But the scribes and Pharisees were filled with rage because Jesus was performing these miracles on the Sabbath. The Sadducees had left earlier because they could not bear to listen to Jesus' sermon. The scribes and Pharisees reasoned amongst themselves, saying, "Now we have a reason to persecute him."

Jesus knew their thoughts. He then saw a man with a withered hand sitting and said to him, "Arise and stand before Me."

As the man stood up, Jesus looked towards the scribes and Pharisees and said, "I will ask you one thing: Is it lawful on the Sabbath, to do good or to do evil, to save life or to destroy?"

He looked around at all of them but none gave Him an answer, so He then turned back to look at the man with the withered hand, saying to him, "Stretch out your hand."

The man did so. The bones started to crack into place, the joints moved into their correct alignment, and so his hand was restored as whole as his other one. The man was grabbing his hand frantically in excitement and began to jump up into the air and laugh. The crowds laughed with him.

Jesus said, speaking to all that were there, "Most assuredly I say to you, they who believe in Me, the works that I do they will do also; And greater works than these they will do. In My name they will cast out demons; they will lay hands on the sick, and they will recover."

Then He noticed a paralysed man who had been brought there lying on a mat, and everyone fell silent. Jesus walked over to him and said, "Your sins are forgiven you."

The scribes and Pharisees were stunned at what they heard Jesus say and reasoned further amongst themselves, saying, "Who is *this* who speaks blasphemies?! Who can forgive sins but God alone?!"

But Jesus perceived their thoughts and He answered them, saying, "Why are you reasoning in your hearts? Which is easier, to say, 'Your sins are forgiven you' or to say 'Rise up and walk'? But that you may know that the Son of God has power on earth to forgive sins."

He looked at the paralysed man and said, "I say to you, arise, pick up your mat, and go home."

Immediately, he rose up before all of them and wept.

Jesus continued, "See, you have been made well. Sin no more, lest a worse thing come upon you."

The man picked up his mat and departed, glorifying God as he went.

The multitude marveled and praised God.

Jesus turned towards the scribes and Pharisees and said to them, "The Sabbath was made for man, and not man for the Sabbath. Therefore, I am Lord of the Sabbath."

The scribes and Pharisees became enraged at Jesus, and so they yelled at Him, "Blasphemy! Blasphemer!"

Jesus continued speaking, "Do not think that I came to destroy the Law or the Prophets. I did not come to destroy but to fulfill."

The scribes and Pharisees turned their backs to Jesus and began to walk away.

Jesus quickly said to them, "You do not have God's word abiding in you, because the One He sent, Him you do not believe."

They all stopped and turned around and the highest ranked

Pharisee walked over to Jesus and said, "Who do you think you are speaking to us in such a manner, and saying such false things about us and yourself?!"

But Jesus answered, "You search the Scriptures, for in them you think you have eternal life; and these are they which testify of Me. But you are not willing to come to Me that you may have life. Most assuredly, I say to you, unless you are born again, you cannot see the kingdom of God, unless you are born of water and of the Spirit, you cannot enter the kingdom of God."

The scribes and Pharisees were shocked at what Jesus had said, then another Pharisee looked around at the crowds and yelled out to them, "Why are you all listening to this blasphemer?!" Then he looked at Jesus and yelled at Him saying, "Why are you saying these things about us?!"

Jesus answered, "You outwardly appear righteous, but inside you are full of hypocrisy and lawlessness. You love the praise of people more than the praise of God and you justify yourselves before others, but God knows your hearts. For what is highly esteemed among people is an abomination in the sight of God."

Then the scribes and Pharisees departed from there because they could no longer bear to listen to what Jesus was saying. The high ranking Pharisee who remained, pointed at Jesus and said to Him, "You will pay for your blasphemy." And once more he turned his back to Jesus and walked away with the rest of the scribes and Pharisees. The soldiers also departed with them.

Jesus looked at the crowd and said, "Can the blind lead the blind?"

The Pharisees knew that He was talking about them, but they did not give Jesus their attention.

He continued, "Will they not both fall into the ditch? And indeed there are last who will be first, and there are first who will be last. And whoever exalts themselves will be humbled, and they who humble themselves will be exalted. God has scattered the proud in the imagination of their hearts. I do not pray for these alone, but also for those who will believe in Me."

When Jesus had finished speaking, He saw four horsemen riding towards Him.

When they arrived at the edge of the crowd a centurion climbed off of his horse and quickly made his way to Jesus. The people wondered what the centurion and his soldiers wanted.

When the centurion arrived before Jesus, he pleaded, "Lord, my servant is lying at home paralysed and dreadfully tormented."

Jesus replied, "I will come and heal him."

The centurion said, "Lord, I am not worthy that you should come under my roof. But only speak a word, and my servant will be healed. For I also am a man under authority, having soldiers under me. I say to this one 'Go', and he goes; and to another, 'Come', and he comes; and to my servant, 'Do this', and he does it."

When Jesus heard the centurion say that, He marveled, and said to the multitude, "Assuredly, I say to you, I have not found such great faith, not even in Israel!"

Then Jesus said to the centurion, "Go your way, as you have believed, so let it be done to you."

His servant was healed at that very moment. The centurion smiled at Jesus, then returned to his horse and rode off with his soldiers.

As the four horsemen rode off, Jesus slowly turned His

head and stared across the sea. A moment passed by and the multitude wondered what He was staring at.

Peter, one of Jesus' twelve Apostles, approached Him and asked, "Master, what is wrong?"

Jesus did not answer him right away. After a moment, He replied, "We must go to the other side of the sea. You and the rest of the Apostles, get in the boat and leave now. God has fed this multitude fish and loaves of bread, they will have enough strength for the long walk home without having to make camp here."

Confused, Peter replied, "Yes Lord."

He went to the other Apostles and told them what Jesus had said to him. Most of them were confused about why Jesus wanted to go across the sea. They also asked how He was to get across if they took the boat and left Him ashore. None of them knew, yet they still obeyed.

The Apostles walked through the crowd and shouted, "The sermon is over, go your way."

The multitude prepared to make their way home, and as they did so, the Apostles climbed into their boat but did not row anywhere yet, because they were still confused and waited to see what Jesus was going to do.

Jesus did not go with them, instead He walked in the opposite direction towards the mountain.

Peter said to the Apostles, "Let us go now."

At this point, Simone did not know what to do or where to go, so she thought to herself, "I will make my way to the back of the crowds and then I will follow Jesus." And that is exactly what she did, keeping her distance.

A short while later, Jesus arrived upon a path and walked along it and Simone followed Him.

Approaching Jesus and Simone from the opposite direction was a procession of people, wearing black. A dead man was being carried to a tomb that had been prepared for him, he was the only son of his mother; and she was also a widow. A large crowd was with her.

When Jesus saw her, He had compassion for her.

Simone saw this as an opportunity to blend in with the crowd, and so she did.

Jesus walked up to the mother, and said, "Do not weep."

This was confusing to her.

Then Jesus went to the dead man.

The people who carried him stood still, Jesus touched the flat frame he was being carried on, and said, "Young man, I say to you, arise."

And he who was dead sat up! He then looked around confused and said, "What is happening?"

Jesus gave him back to his mother.

She was overcome with fear and joy, yet she threw her arms around her son and wept, saying, "Thank you God!" repeatedly.

Fear came upon all of them, and they praised and worshiped God, glorifying Him, saying, "A great Prophet has risen up amongst us" and "God has visited His people!"

When they became silent, Jesus said to them, "Concerning the dead, that they rise, God spoke to Moses saying, 'I Am the God of Abraham, the God of Isaac, and the God of Jacob'. He is not the God of the dead, but the God of the living."

And so, they all continued to praise and worship God.

Then they turned around and walked back the way they had come.

Jesus stood still, smiling, and watched the people leaving, and saw Simone standing near looking at Him as people walked between and around them. When the crowd had finally left, Simone did not know what to do or what to say, so she asked the first thing she thought of, "Lord, after all that I have witnessed You doing, I am sure that You know something about 'the book'."

Jesus smiled and said, "Yes Simone, I know everything about 'the book'."

Still smiling, He continued, "Follow Me, and I will tell you all about it and what must take place in your generation."

That statement made Simone very curious.

Jesus began to walk off of the path and up the mountain, Simone followed.

She thought, the fact that she was walking and talking with Jesus was very surreal. She also realised that her whole journey was God's doing and so she felt safe from then on.

Jesus spoke, saying, "Simone, God chose to give 'the book' to you for a greater purpose, which I will explain to you on our way back down the mountain."

Jesus continued, "You have travelled to many countries in your life, but the country that you thought of on your way to the library was Macedonia, and that is where My Father chose for you to begin your journey. You do not have to die in order to return home, just close your eyes and say 'Return', there is power in the spoken word, but do not do that now for I have much to tell you."

Jesus stopped and so did Simone, "Stay here Simone, I must go to pray" He said.

Jesus walked a little further away from her and began to pray. At this point, as she watched Jesus praying her mind flooded with thoughts, "What is He going to tell me?.. It must be of significant importance that God would allow me to experience history."

All of a sudden, she gasped in fear and fell back. Jesus transfigured before her eyes, His face shone brighter than the sun, and His clothes glistened becoming as white as the light.

And then Moses and Elijah appeared in glory and spoke with Jesus, but Simone could not hear what they were saying.

Greatly afraid, she did not know what to do.

Then, a cloud came and overshadowed them and the surrounding area, and a voice came out of the cloud, saying, "This is My beloved Son, in whom I am well pleased. Listen to Him!"

Simone knew that she was being spoken to, she became very fearful and closed her eyes.

Jesus said to her, "Arise Simone, and do not fear."

Then, Simone opened her eyes and only saw Jesus, not transfigured but in His human form.

She slowly stood up and Jesus said to her, "Let us go now, My Apostles will be in need and will be calling out to Me in a while."

Simone was puzzled because she did not know what He was talking about. And so they headed back down the mountain.

Jesus said to Simone, "Listen carefully Simone, and remember what I am about to tell you, for you must warn My people of what is to come. Your generation has taken My words very lightly. You are living in the end times Simone."

When she heard that, her blood ran cold and she shuddered. Then she asked Jesus, "Lord, when will the end come?"

Jesus paused a moment and then answered, "Of that day and hour no one knows, not even the angels of heaven, but My Father only. For it will come as a snare on all those who dwell on the face of the earth. Watch therefore, be ready and pray, for I will arrive at an hour you do not expect. As it was in the days of Noah, so it will be also in the days of the Son of God: They ate, they drank, they married, until the day that Noah entered the ark, and the flood came and took them all away. Likewise as it was in the days of Lot: They ate, they drank, they bought, they sold, they planted, they built: but on the day that Lot went out of Sodom it rained fire and brimstone from heaven and destroyed them all. So also will My second coming be. And you will hear of wars and rumours of wars. See that you are not troubled; for all these things must come to pass, but the end is not yet. For nation will rise against nation, and kingdom against kingdom. And there will be further famines, pestilences, and earthquakes in various places. All these are the beginning of sorrows. Yes, the time has come that whoever kills you will think that they offer God service. And because iniquity will abound, the love of many will grow cold. Then they will deliver you up to tribulation and kill you, and you will be hated by all nations for My names sake. For then there will be a great tribulation, such as has not been since the beginning of the world until this time, no, nor ever shall be. And if those days were not shortened, no flesh would be saved; but for the elect's sake those days will be shortened. Then if anyone says to you 'Look, here is the Christ!' or 'There!' do not believe it. For false christs and prophets will rise and show great signs and wonders to deceive, if possible, even the elect."

Jesus continued, "See, I have told you beforehand. Therefore if they say to you 'Look, He is in the desert!' do not go out; or 'Look, He is in the inner rooms!' do not believe it. For as lightening comes from the east and flashes to the west, so also will My arrival be. Immediately after the tribulation of those days the sun will be darkened, and the moon will not give its light; the stars will fall from heaven and, the powers of the heavens will be shaken. Then My sign will appear in heaven, and then all the nations of the earth will mourn, and they will see Me arriving with all the holy angels on the clouds of heaven with power and great glory. And I will send My angels with a great sound of a trumpet, and they will gather together My elect from one end of heaven to the other. And they will also gather all things that offend, and those who practice iniquity, and will cast them into the furnace of fire. And this will be preached in all the world as a witness to all the nations, and then the end will come. Assuredly, I say to you, your generation will by no means pass away until all these things take place."

Simone was shocked and overwhelmed. She had many questions to ask Jesus about what He had said but she was speechless and fearful.

Simone realised they had arrived at the spot where she had first appeared in the chapter. She asked Jesus, "Lord, do I return home now?"

"No," He replied, "there is one more thing you must witness. I want you to see and know the reality of your enemy. The devil and his legions. I saw satan fall like lightening from heaven. He was a murderer from the beginning, and does not stand in the truth, because there is no truth in him. When he speaks a lie, he speaks from his own resources, for he is a liar and the father of lies."

Simone became frightened as Jesus continued, "Do not fear Simone, tell the people I give them authority over all the power of the enemy. In My name they will cast out demons."

Simone did not fear anymore because those words gave her comfort and reassurance.

Jesus then said, "Simone, I will send you over the sea and when you arrive there do not move from that place. I will be there soon and when I look at you that is when you are to return home. Now I must go to My Apostles for they are in peril."

Simone remembered seeing the Apostles cast off out to sea and when she looked out over the water there was a mighty cloud above it. As she watched, a glow of white light covered her body and suddenly she took off from the ground and rocketed over the sea, with a shout of joy, knowing that she was safe because God was in control.

She entered into the cloud and saw the Apostles screaming and panicked. Their boat was filling with water and they were being thrown around by the waves because of the windstorm.

At the same time John, one of the Apostles, looked up and saw a 'white light' shooting across the dark grey sky and yelled out, "What is that?!" pointing towards Simone.

Some of the disciples heard him and so they looked up as well but they did not see anything.

Then, James, the brother of John, yelled out to him, saying, "What was it John?!"

John, bewildered, replied, "Never mind!"

And so they tended to their dilemma.

Simone arrived on the other side of the sea behind a large tomb. She did not know what she was doing there but she knew that she had to wait. And so she leant back on the tomb and within seconds she fell asleep, exhausted from all that had happened that day.

Back at sea, the Apostles were still unable to take control of their situation. And at that time, James saw a figure walking towards them on the water and then he pointed and yelled out, "Look! It's a ghost!"

And they cried out in fear, immediately the 'ghost' spoke to them saying, "Do not fear, it is I, Jesus!"

They all marveled. Then Peter asked Jesus, "Lord, if it is You, command me to come to You on the water!"

Jesus replied, "Come!"

And when Peter had climbed out of the boat, he walked on the water to go to Jesus. But, when he took his eyes off of Jesus he saw that the wind was wild and rough, he became afraid and began to sink.

So he yelled out, "Lord! Save me!"

And immediately, Jesus stretched out His hand and caught Peter, and then said to him, "You of little faith, why did you doubt?"

Peter did not answer and so they walked across the water to the boat and climbed into it.

Then Judas Iscariot grabbed Jesus by the arm and said, "Teacher, do You not care that we are perishing?!"

Then, Jesus rebuked the wind saying to it, "Peace, be still!" and the wind ceased and there was a great calm.

Jesus said to them, "Why are you so fearful?.. Where is your faith?"

His Apostles marveled, saying, "Even the winds and the sea obey Him."

Peter said, "Truly You are the Son of God."

Jesus spoke, "Let us continue the journey, for dusk is upon us."

They were not far from their destination. Jesus took the opportunity to talk to His Apostles about the events that were soon to take place, saying, "A little while longer and the world will see Me no more. When we go to Jerusalem I will be betrayed to the elders and the chief priests, and they will condemn Me to death, and deliver Me to the gentiles to mock, and to scourge, and to spit upon. They will crucify Me and on the third day I will rise again. And when I am lifted up from the earth, I will draw all peoples to Myself."

The Apostles were shocked, and Peter said, "Lord, we don't have to go to Jerusalem."

Then John said, "We will hide You."

Jesus replied, speaking to all of them, "I have spoken to all of you about this, thus it was written, and thus it is necessary for Me to suffer and give My life as a ransom for many, and to rise from the dead the third day."

The Apostles knew that but they did not know that it would be so soon. Jesus continued, "All authority has been given to Me in heaven and on earth. Go therefore and make disciples of all the nations, baptising them in the name of the Father and of the Son and of the Holy Spirit. Teaching them to observe all things that I have commanded you and that repentance and remission of sins should be preached in My name to all nations, beginning in Jerusalem. They who hear you hear Me, they who reject you reject Me, and they who reject Me reject He who sent Me."

"The Helper, the Holy Spirit," Jesus said, "who God will send in My name, He will teach you all things, and bring to your remembrance all of the things that I have said to you. The Spirit of truth who proceeds from God, He will testify of Me."

Jesus paused, looked around at them and smiled, "Rejoice because your names are written in heaven! In My Father's house are many mansions; if it were not so, I would have told you. I go to prepare a place for you. I am with you, even to the end of the age."

When He had finished speaking they arrived at the shore. There were many tombs there, both opened and sealed. The Apostles climbed out of the boat and a moment later Jesus did too.

As soon as His feet touched the land a bone chilling scream was heard from inside a tomb in the distance.

The Apostles looked towards the direction of the scream and were troubled.

Simone woke up in a fright, because the tomb against which she was sleeping was the tomb from which the scream came from. She stood up and was about to peek around the side of the tomb when all of a sudden a man stormed out screaming, and ran towards Jesus and His Apostles.

The man had cuts all over his body that he had inflicted upon himself with sharp stones. His eyes were black. He was very dirty, wore rags and lived in the tombs. No one could bind him, not even with shackles and chains, for he would pull them apart.

Then Jesus walked in front of His Apostles, but Peter ran

out in front of Him and blocked Jesus so that the man could not get to Him.

But Jesus put His hand on Peter's shoulder and said, "Get behind Me."

Peter looked at Jesus and then he stepped back. The Apostles became fearful as the man got closer to them.

When he arrived he fell at Jesus' feet.

The man was scared because he knew that he could not do anything to Jesus and thought that by his screams he could make them flee the area.

Then the man said, in a loud, frightful voice, "What do you want from me, Jesus, Son of the Most High God?! I beg You, do not torment me!"

The Apostles realised that the voice they were hearing was not the man's, rather a demon's that had possessed him.

Jesus was looking at the man, yet He spoke to the demon, "What is your name?"

He answered, saying, "My name is.." Suddenly, many demons were heard from within the man saying, "Legion! For we are many!"

Jesus replied, "Come out of the man, unclean spirits!"

Then the demons said, "We beg You! Do not command us to go into the abyss!"

A large herd of swine were feeding there near the mountains. The legion of demons begged Jesus, "Send us to the swine, that we may enter them!"

Jesus gave them permission. Then, the demons went out of the man and entered the swine, there were about two thousand of them. The herd ran violently down the steep place into the sea, and drowned.

The man from whom the demons had departed sat at Jesus' feet, clothed and in his right mind.

Now the Apostles understood why Jesus had been staring out across the sea earlier at the sermon.

Simone saw the whole event and was looking at Jesus, He also looked back at her and smiled. She smiled in response, then she closed her eyes and said, "Return."

Simone found herself back at her apartment sitting on the floor, this time the force did not throw her back because her departure from history had not been a violent one.

She lied down overcome with emotions and began to cry, speaking aloud, "Thank You God! Thank You for sending Jesus!"

Simone stopped crying and wiped her tears away, then looked at the book and smiled. She sat up next to it, the same curiosity now even stronger pushing her to experience the following chapter.

She took a deep breath and turned the page over revealing the next chapter..

Chapter Four

THE CRUSADES

*J*erusalem, 11th Century AD.. The Christian-friendly Fatimid Muslims of Egypt ruled most of the Holy Land. The Seljuk Muslims of Turkey attacked and overthrew the Fatimids. The Seljuks were not so Christian-friendly, raping and slaughtering the Christians and not allowing them to worship in Jerusalem.

This prompted the Byzantine Emperor, Alexius I Comnenus, in Constantinople, to write a letter to Pope Urban II, in Rome, urging and pleading to him for help.

The Pope summoned a multitude of lords and knights. His cardinals, archbishops, bishops, and priests were all there as well.

The Pope gave a speech about what Alexius had written to him. Everyone present was appalled and with great shouts agreed to take up arms and go on a crusade to avenge those killed and tortured and to place Jerusalem in Christian hands.

The shouting continued, shouts of rage against the Seljuks

and shouts of excitement at the thought of slaying them in the near future.

A person from the crowd yelled out, "God wills it!"

And then everybody joined in chanting, "God wills it!" repeatedly.

It took almost a year for the word to spread throughout Europe. For princes, lords and knights to prepare, recruit and assemble their armies.

And they were:

- Godfrey of Bouillon, Duke of Lower Lorraine. A bold, courageous man and a great leader. His younger brother, Baldwin the Scholar also accompanied him.
- Bohemond, Prince of Otranto and Taranto, today known as Prince of Antioch. A gallant giant, brave, courageous, quick-tempered and a very complicated man. His young nephew, Tancred, also accompanied him. He shared most of his uncle's qualities but was also a generous person.
- Raymond IV, Count of Toulouse. Friendly, good-natured and amusing. He was the eldest crusade leader.
- Robert, Duke of Normandy. Displayed most of Raymond's qualities.
- Hugh, Count of Vermandois. Disrespectful, prideful, self-important person that lacked the qualities of a leader and those of a warrior.

The armies were gathered and were now ready to set off on the crusade to the Holy Land, via Constantinople.

Pope Urban II appointed Bishop Adhemar to lead the crusaders.

The crusade began..

Simone found herself walking in a palace garden. She wore a flowing white dress. As she walked she passed by people and all who passed bowed their heads to her.

Simone figured out that she must be an important person and so she raised her hand and said, "Stop" to a man walking by.

The man stopped with his head bowed, Simone continued, "Who do you say that I am?"

The man was puzzled, yet quickly answered, "You are Anna Comnena, Daughter of Emperor Alexius."

Simone was surprised and excited, because she knew the history of the Crusades and also knew from what she had just read that the crusaders had not yet arrived.

She knew that it was going to be an extraordinary sight and was thrilled that she was going to witness their spectacular and eventful arrival into Constantinople.

Simone dismissed him and quickly rushed into the palace, entering a great hall where she saw Alexius sitting on his throne reading a letter.

Alexius saw Simone and said to her, "Anna, come here."

Simone replied giggling, "Yes father" and quickly made her way to him.

Alexius said to her, "Count Hugh will be the first of the crusaders to arrive by sea. Listen to the letter he sent to me ahead of his arrival, 'Know, O Emperor, that I am king of kings, and superior to all who are under the heavens. I give you permission to greet me on my arrival, and with magnificence receive me as befits my noble birth.'"

Simone and Alexius looked at each other and then burst out with laughter.

Horns were sounded outside from the towers. A servant walked into the hall and up to the Emperor, head bowed.

Alexius said, "Speak."

"Great Emperor," he said, "Hugh is in sight and is approaching the harbour." He paused, slowly looked up at Alexius and continued, "It does not look good, your Eminence."

Alexius stood up and walked to the balcony, throwing Hugh's letter into a fireplace on his way out. Simone joined him.

They saw the remaining few battered ships Hugh was sailing in on. Most of his army had been lost at sea.

A demeaning and undignified arrival.

Hugh and his remaining army were transported to the palace court. Many shouted praises at them along the way and they were showered with gifts when they arrived at the court.

"Count Hugh!.." the Emperor exclaimed, "Welcome to Constantinople!" he continued, trying to ease his mood.

Hugh replied, "Thank you for your hospitality Emperor, but I wish it were a 'well come'."

Alexius said, "I will replenish your weaponry and food, but I cannot replace your brave men." He continued, "Come now to your quarters, they have been lavishly prepared, and my servants will attend to your every need."

That quickly put a smile on Hugh's face.

Alexius ordered that Hugh's army be fed and taken outside of Constantinople's walls to set up camp because there would not be enough space to accommodate all of the armies within the walls.

Hugh and his army were kept under close watch at all times, just as the other crusaders were to be treated in the same manner.

Hugh did not mind being watched because of the luxurious way in which he was being treated.

Emperor Alexius did not trust any of the crusade leaders and that was why he required them to pledge their allegiance and give their oath over the *alleged* 'crown of thorns', that as they set out on the crusade they would give all of the land they seized to Alexius.

Hugh had no problem in being a 'liege' for Alexius and that was why, one night, at the palace court surrounded by a great gathering of people including Simone, Hugh took the oath and pledged his allegiance to the Emperor over the 'crown of thorns'.

Alexius smiled, he and Hugh embraced, the people cheered and the celebrations continued all through the night.

The following day, Godfrey and his army arrived. The Emperor was informed and so he made his way to the palace court. Simone was present also.

Once again, the new arrivals were escorted to the court, with shouts of praise from the people along the way, and were presented with gifts from the Emperor.

Alexius ordered the servants to bring food for Godfrey and his men.

Alexius said, "Welcome, Duke Godfrey. It is an honour to meet the legendary 'Godfrey'!"

Godfrey smiled and said, "Thank you Emperor."

Alexius continued, "Come now to your quarters, they have been lavishly prepared and my servants will attend to your every need."

Godfrey replied, "Again, thank you Emperor, but I will set up camp with my army and I will stay in my tent."

That made Alexius even more cautious of Godfrey. Fearing that he may not take an oath, Alexius ordered that Godfrey be watched more than the others.

Godfrey had already given an oath of allegiance to his German Emperor, Henry.

The whole situation had the potential to turn ugly.

Alexius reluctantly ordered that Godfrey and his army be taken to the site where they would be setting up camp, not far from Hugh's army.

After they had had their fair share of food and drink, they pitched their tents and rested until the next day.

Later that evening, an ambassador was sent to Godfrey by the Emperor. When he approached him he said, "Sir Godfrey, Emperor Alexius summons you to his court."

Godfrey did not reply, but turned his head and stared at the palace, knowing very well why he was being summoned.

He ignored the ambassador and leapt onto his horse making his way to the court where there were many gathered, including Simone and Hugh.

Alexius was sitting in his chair and motioned with his hand for Godfrey to approach him.

Godfrey made his way to Alexius through the clear and straight path before him.

Everyone stopped talking as their attention was drawn to Godfrey. When he approached Alexius, looking straight at him, the Emperor simply asked, "Duke Godfrey, will you take an oath of allegiance to me?"

Godfrey looked at the floor and let out a large sigh, then he looked up at Alexius and answered, "Emperor, you know very well that I have already taken an oath of allegiance to Emperor Henry. I will not be dishonouring that oath by breaking my word and making a new one."

Now the people began to talk and whisper amongst themselves.

Alexius raised his hand and everybody fell silent. Alexius, staring at Godfrey, replied, "Godfrey, how can you be trusted if you do not become a 'liege' to me? We must settle this matter before you set off to the Holy Land."

Godfrey replied, "My word is enough, I can be trusted and we *will* settle this matter."

Then Godfrey turned and walked away. The people watched on in disbelief.

The Emperor was furious, yet kept silent because he knew that he needed Godfrey and that Godfrey could start a war against him with the other armies.

When Godfrey arrived back at camp, he noticed that Alexius' servants were leaving his camp and were heading back inside the city walls. The army wondered why they did so in such a rush, but Godfrey knew why.

The following morning there were no servants tending to

Godfrey and his army. They could see in the distance in the next camp over that Hugh's army was being tended to.

Godfrey then made his way to the Emperor. When he arrived at the palace he saw Simone and asked her sternly, "Where is Alexius?!"

Simone looked at Godfrey for a moment, smiled and pointed to the throne room.

Godfrey did not say a word but quickly made his way to the throne. As he walked away from Simone he looked back at her and smiled.

Once he had turned his head back, Simone quickly yet quietly followed him and hid behind the columns.

As he arrived at the entry of the throne room, he kicked the door open and calmly walked towards Alexius.

The Emperor's Imperial Guards stood in front of Alexius in an attempt to block Godfrey from getting to him, but he did not stop.

Alexius yelled, "Let him pass!" to his guards, and so they did.

When Godfrey approached, he said, "What is the meaning of this?!"

Acting innocent Alexius replied, "Meaning of what?"

Godfrey was not a person to be made a fool of. He stared at Alexius, then smiled and walked away.

Simone was at the entry but she hid back behind a column as Godfrey came out.

When Godfrey arrived back at camp he told Baldwin to tell the army to prepare for battle. Baldwin thought that an enemy must be approaching Constantinople, and that they were going to take part in protecting the city.

So Baldwin asked Godfrey, "Who is coming? The Seljuks?"

Godfrey, knowing Baldwin's thoughts, replied, "No Brother, we are the enemy!"

Baldwin was bewildered as Godfrey continued, "We have travelled from afar, scaled cliffs, climbed mountains and crossed through harsh deserts. My men did not die just so that we could come here and be denied food and drink from the very person who pleaded for our help!"

Baldwin was shocked at Godfrey's words, and feeling so dishonoured himself, he yelled, "Prepare for battle!"

The whole army erupted and the shout was heard all throughout Constantinople.

Emperor Alexius realised then just how far he had pushed Godfrey. He quickly ordered his generals to prepare his Imperial Army, and he himself went to Hugh's chambers and said to him, "Go to Godfrey immediately and tell him that I am willing to modify the oath to suit both of us. If not, this will only end in bloodshed, and may even be the end of the crusade itself."

Hugh did not delay and quickly made his way to Godfrey's camp.

When he arrived he approached Godfrey and pleaded with him saying, "Godfrey, I bid you, stop this. The Emperor has proposed to modify the oath to suit the both of you. If you take the oath he will give us everything we need. We must obey him, otherwise matters will turn out poorly for us. An attack on the Emperor will only end in death."

Godfrey looked at Hugh with a skeptical frown and questioned him, "Alexius himself told you that he will modify the oath?"

Hugh answered, "Yes, it was he that told me."

Godfrey looked at Baldwin for a moment and said, "Tell the men to stand down."

Baldwin smiled at Godfrey and replied, "Wise decision Brother."

"Indeed" Hugh added.

Godfrey said to Hugh, "Tell Alexius that I accept."

Hugh departed at once to inform the Emperor.

The Emperor wasted no time after Hugh delivered the message. Once more, he sent one of his ambassadors to formally invite Godfrey to the palace court so that he may give his oath that very night.

To make the deal sweeter, Alexius even sent a chariot to carry Godfrey to the court.

Godfrey and Baldwin were realising the type of man Alexius really was, but to avoid disrespecting him further, Godfrey climbed on the chariot and said to Baldwin, "Come with me Brother."

Godfrey grabbed the reins and said to the driver, "Get off." Then Baldwin climbed on.

When they arrived at the court a multitude of people were there once more, including Simone and Hugh.

They all became silent and stared at Godfrey and Baldwin.

They both approached Alexius, who was sitting in his chair, and in front of him the *alleged* 'crown of thorns'.

Baldwin stopped just behind Godfrey.

Alexius spoke loudly saying, "Duke Godfrey, will you honour my life and everything that belongs to me?"

Godfrey did not answer immediately and everybody was anxious.

After a moment, He responded, "I will."

Alexius replied, "Well then Godfrey, pledge your allegiance over the blessed Crown of Thorns."

Godfrey looked at the alleged relic and spoke out aloud, "I, Godfrey, will honour the Emperor's life and everything that belongs to him."

The people cheered, but Godfrey and Baldwin did not want to be part of the celebrations so they departed and headed back to camp.

Alexius was relieved, the reason why he modified the oath and sped up the whole ceremony was because he had received word that Bohemond was approaching the city, and if Godfrey and he had joined forces they would have posed a great threat to the Emperor.

Alexius had no doubt that Bohemond would attack if need be, because he and Alexius had clashed in the past and Bohemond had seized some of the Byzantine Empire's land.

Even though now they were on the same side, Alexius and Raymond, one of the crusade leaders, were very suspicious of Bohemond.

The following morning Bohemond and his army arrived. When the Emperor was informed he walked out onto a balcony where Simone was sitting. In her hands was a stylus and some parchment, and she was looking out over the city.

Alexius noticed that she was writing something, and so he asked her, "What are you writing my precious?"

Simone looked at him and answered, "A biography of your reign as Emperor, Father. I am calling it 'The Alexiad'."

Alexius smiled at her approvingly and she smiled back.

Then, Alexius turned to see Bohemond arriving. His smile quickly turned into worry because he saw Bohemond and his army heading to Godfrey's camp and not to the gates of the city.

That made Alexius restless. He knew that Godfrey would not attack because he took the oath, and that he is a man of his word. But Bohemond had not yet taken the oath.

Alexius, and many others were unsure if he even would.

Bohemond's motives were unclear to everyone, including the other crusade leaders.

Godfrey however was not concerned, because he and Bohemond had great respect for one another.

When Bohemond spotted Godfrey he climbed off of his horse and they greeted each other. Bohemond asked Godfrey, "Is what I hear true?"

Godfrey knew what he was referring to and answered bluntly, "Yes."

Bohemond grinned cheekily, then turned to face his men and yelled with a mighty voice, "This day, Constantinople will be ours! Prepare for battle!"

His army cheered, the roar was heard all throughout the city, even reaching the Emperor's ears.

Simone said to Alexius, "Father, do not fret. They will not attack."

Alexius looked at Simone and replied asking, "How do you know this Anna?"

Simone did not know how to answer, so she just stared back at him blankly.

Then, Alexius summoned his generals and told them to prepare his army.

Bohemond turned to Godfrey and said to him, "I will kill the Emperor myself."

Bohemond looked at Godfrey's army and asked, "Why is your army not ready to do battle?"

Godfrey approached Bohemond and grabbed him by the shoulders getting his attention, "Bohemond, I have given Alexius an oath of allegiance! I have given him my word!"

Bohemond's excitement quickly turned to disappointment.

Godfrey continued, "Our crown is Jerusalem, not Constantinople. Our enemy is the Seljuks, not the Byzantines."

Bohemond considered Alexius as his enemy, yet for the sake of the crusade a truce had to be formed. Bohemond turned reluctantly towards his army and shouted, "Stand down and disarm!.. Constantinople will have to wait!"

Emperor Alexius breathed a sigh of relief as he watched Bohemond's army disarm. Alexius turned to Simone and said, "Anna, you were right" and then smiled at her.

Escorts were sent to Bohemond to take him and his army to the palace court so that he may be officially welcomed, but Bohemond sent them back.

The Emperor, not wanting the situation to escalate further, ordered his servants to take gifts, food and drink to Bohemond and his men.

Bohemond would not eat the Emperor's food nor did he drink his wine, fearing that it could be poisoned, yet his army did not share the same concern and so they ate the Emperor's food like wild beasts.

Alexius was informed that Bohemond was not eating nor was he drinking. That offended the Emperor and he growled angrily, "What insolence!"

He told one of his ambassadors to go to Bohemond and inform him that he was expected to pledge his allegiance that very night.

The ambassador did so. When he approached Bohemond he said to him, "Prince Bohemond, Emperor Alexius requests that you join him in the palace court this evening where you will be required to become a liege of the great Emperor."

Bohemond let out a great laugh and told the ambassador, "Tell your 'Great Emperor' that I will be there."

The ambassador was confused and surprised by his answer as he had been expecting a certain degree of rebelliousness.

The ambassador reported back to Alexius. The Emperor was bewildered by what he was told, yet still remained cautious.

Now Bohemond's motives were even more unclear making Alexius more apprehensive.

When evening came Alexius sent a chariot to Bohemond.

Bohemond thought it would be amusing to himself if he rode into Constantinople on a Byzantine chariot with his army behind him, and so he did, telling the driver, "Hand over the reins and get off!"

He told Tancred, his nephew, to join him on the chariot and so he did. He also told his knights to follow him to the court.

At the court, the Emperor was at his seat and a large crowd of people were gathered, including Simone and Hugh.

They were all anxious to hear what Bohemond would say, except for Simone of course, because she already knew what was going to take place.

The crowd fell silent when they felt the ground tremble beneath them. Their attention was diverted to Bohemond and his knights marching to the court.

When they arrived, Bohemond stepped off of the chariot and with giant steps and an unbowed head he approached the Emperor.

Alexius, at this point, was firmly grasping the armrests of his seat. It was the first time the two had faced each other in such close proximity.

Alexius was astonished by the giant Norman's size.

Bohemond could not be pleased or amused so easily, so he kept his usual straight and serious expression.

Alexius felt agitated, yet for his sake he could not appear to be so in front of his people, and so he calmly asked Bohemond, with a loud voice, "Prince Bohemond, what moved you to take up this crusade?"

Bohemond grinned, replying but without answering his question directly, "I am here of my own will as an ally to the Byzantine Empire!"

At that moment it was as if the world had stopped spinning. No one could believe what they had just heard.

Alexius and his men however were unfazed as they knew of Bohemond's true cunning character.

So Alexius replied, pointing at the *alleged* 'crown of thorns', saying, "Well, in that case you will have no difficulty in pledging your oath to me over the Crown of Thorns."

Bohemond did not care about relics and so he smirked

saying, "I, Bohemond, pledge my allegiance to the Byzantine Empire."

Alexius responded, "And will you, Prince Bohemond, surrender to me every piece of land that you seize from here to Jerusalem, and Jerusalem itself?"

Bohemond smirked again, and replied, "I will."

Now everyone was in shock at Bohemond's meekness. This was out of character for the 'Great Bohemond' that everyone had heard stories of.

At that moment everybody cheered. Alexius and his men were not falling for Bohemond's 'act', but the Emperor had a plan of his own.

He stood up and everybody became silent. Looking around at the people, Alexius said, "Continue the celebrations without us for a moment."

Alexius looked at Bohemond and said to him, motioning to his side, "Join me, Bohemond."

Bohemond joined him without hesitation.

Simone followed close behind.

Alexius took Bohemond before a great steel and wooden door with a guard at either side. Alexius motioned to his guards to open the door, as it was heavy and both of them were needed to open it.

It was the treasure hall. Bohemond was astonished, he had never seen so much treasure in all of his life.

After a moment of stunned admiration he said, "If I possessed such treasure I would have become the ruler of the world."

Alexius laughed and said to Bohemond, "A portion of this is yours if you keep your oath."

Bohemond produced the greatest smile he had ever produced.

In that way Emperor Alexius purchased Bohemond's allegiance. No other crusade leader was offered nor given such an amount of treasure.

Bohemond, still smiling, turned to Alexius saying, "I accept your 'gift'."

Then he, Tancred and his knights returned to their camp.

Alexius breathed a sigh of relief, and as he walked back to the celebrations he was approached by a messenger.

Simone was hiding behind a column.

Alexius said, "Speak."

The messenger said, with his head bowed, "Your Eminence, Raymond of Toulouse is approaching and Duke Robert of Normandy is not far behind him."

"Marvelous" Alexius replied.

Simone, also hearing the messenger's announcement came out from behind the column and walked over to Alexius, pleading with him, "Father, may I speak with you? I have a message that I must deliver to you."

Alexius looked at her in confusion and asked, "Message?" He paused then continued angrily, saying, "Anna, who dares to make you a messenger?!"

Simone answered, "God."

Amused, Alexius replied, asking, "Have you drunk much wine tonight?"

"No Father" answered Simone.

Alexius grabbed Simone by the shoulders and said to her, "Anna, have you gone mad?"

Simone answered, "No Father, please hear the message."

Alexius loved his daughter dearly and so he said to her, "Fine, but do not tell anybody that God speaks to you, do you want people to think that you are mad?"

Simone replied, "I do not care what people think of me, I care what God thinks of me."

Alexius said, "Anna stop this at once. Now let us go in the garden and you may tell me this message and then never speak of it again."

So they both went into the garden. Alexius told the guards to clear everybody from there, and so they did.

Then he told the guards to leave, and when they had, he said to Simone, "Now Anna, let me hear this message. I will hear the whole message and then I will speak once you have finished delivering it."

Simone took a deep breath and began to speak, "Father, countless numbers of innocent lives have been lost at the hands of the five crusader armies on their journeys here to Constantinople, and many more will be lost on the way to the Holy Land. Raymond and Robert are yet to arrive and they too will become lieges of yours but because of false information that you will receive of a battle in Antioch, involving Bohemond, your army will turn from helping him and in this way the loyalty and oaths that have been pledged to you shall be broken. The crusaders will claim everything for themselves and their churches. As I speak, the Fatimids are recapturing Jerusalem from the Seljuks and all Christians will once more be allowed to worship there."

Simone paused for a moment, and then continued, "This crusade was established to war against the Seljuks, but it will instead attack the Christian-friendly Fatimids, and in this way all Muslims will unite against all Christians if you allow the crusade to continue. Raymond will return home, but before that, he will become the leader of the crusade because Bishop Adhemar has been wounded and will die. Bohemond will conquer and become Prince of Antioch. Godfrey will become ruler of Jerusalem and his brother Baldwin will succeed him as king, but first, Baldwin will become Prince of Edessa. Hugh will return home even before he reaches Jerusalem. Robert will follow soon after."

"This will not be the only crusade, there will be nine in total and they will last almost two centuries. The crusades will birth a special order of knights called the Templars, and the Hospitallers. The nine crusades will see noble and evil men, both Christian and Muslim alike. A great and mighty King of English descent will come from France and strike fear and respect into the hearts of every Muslim, and they shall call him 'the one with the heart of a lion'. He shall ride his war horse before the army of the great 'merciful' Muslim leader and not one will attack him. In the end it will all be for nothing. The Muslims will reclaim the Holy Land and it will remain in their hands for many centuries until God gives it to the Jewish people."

Alexius was stunned speechless, his eyes wide from shock. He could not believe what he had just heard. Then it was as if he regained consciousness, and he spoke, "Anna, my beautiful Anna" he said and then continued, "You have surely gone mad. I forbid you to tell anybody what you have just told me."

Simone replied, "I am not mad Father, I bring you the truth."

Alexius was enraged and slapped Simone on the cheek. She

put her hands to her face and Alexius yelled at her, quoting the crusaders, "God wills it!"

Simone looked at Alexius with tears in her eyes and yelled back at him, "God does NOT will it!" She then ran to her chambers, closed the door and leant back against it.

She began to cry and fell to her knees, then she looked up and said, "God, forgive them for they do not know what they do."

After a moment, she said, "I will not be part of this any further."

She closed her eyes and said, "Return."

Simone was instantaneously taken back home.

She slumped down on the floor, still sobbing and called out to God, "Lord, forgive me! I tried! I tried!"

She sat there bitterly for a while contemplating what she had just experienced.

After a moment she realised that all the sadness, regret and bitterness in the world could not change what had happened, and so she resolved to move on.

She wasted no time in turning the page over to reveal the next chapter..

Chapter Five

1666

London was still gripped by a great plague unseen since the infamous bubonic plague, the Black Death, of the 1340s which had claimed the lives of more than 75 million people.

The present plague had the same symptoms as the Black Death which was black and/or red patches, inflamed lymph glands of buboes on the neck, in the armpits and in the groin, swollen gums, painful headaches, vomiting, and delirium right before death. Delirium to the point where a mother or father would take the lives of their own children in their insanity.

For the sick, the pain was unbearable and so some jumped out of windows, some drowned themselves, some shot themselves, and others found all sorts of ways to take their own lives. Yet most vented their pain with endless and dreadful groaning. Nobody approached to console them fearing death themselves. The sick called out for death, yet they did not find it when they pleased, rather, it took them when it pleased.

The people thought it to be Divine vengeance, and so they confessed all sorts of sins to God, from thievery to adultery and murder. And yet they ran to psychics and fortune-tellers, and to all sorts of other deceivers who fed their fears such as witches and wizards who claimed to have 'the cure'.. for a price.

The people flocked to them and were poisoned. There was no cure for them but death.

In doing all of these things the people mocked God. They were right, judgment *was* upon Europe.

An exception was the Bavarian town of Oberammergau, its residents vowed that if God spared them from the plague, they would stage a play every ten years for all time. It would depict the life, death, resurrection, and ascension of Jesus Christ.

Miraculously, God did spare them.

In London, death ruled in every corner of the city and everyone thought of their graves.

It was the second day of September, and Simone found herself in a small room lying in a bed, looking at a wall dimly lit by a candle.

There was a very strong yet pleasant smell of baked bread.

Taking a moment, she thought about what she had just read and realised that she was most likely in London in the midst of the great plague.

She was not fearful of contracting the plague because she knew that, unlike the residents of London, she had an 'escape'.

Regardless, she was very apprehensive about experiencing this chapter.

As she stared at the wall, a black rat ran across the floor. Simone screeched and jumped up.

She recalled how the plague had spread. It was the fleas that fed off of the black rats that picked up the bacteria, 'Yersinia pestis', which was then spread into humans when the fleas fed off of them.

She saw a broom in the corner of the small room and ran towards it. The rat was startled because it heard and felt the vibrations of Simone running and so it also ran.

It escaped through the slightly open door and into the kitchen.

Simone was right behind it, broom in hand, but when she arrived at the kitchens entry she stopped abruptly.

She saw six black rats eating from a loaf of bread on the table.

The kitchen was very well lit because the fire that heated the large ovens was still burning strongly.

Simone knew that she had to kill the rats because they most likely harboured fleas infected with the plague bacteria, yet the broom she was holding was not going to do.

She closed the kitchen door, ran over to the fire and grabbed a large smoldering log from it, then she ran over to the table and crushed a rat with it burning it in the process.

The other five rats scattered but Simone moved quickly and managed to crush another one.

Now there were four of them squeaking and running erratically around in the kitchen.

Simone killed two more, as the servant of the house got up out of bed to see what all the commotion was about.

He opened the door to the kitchen and the other two rats

escaped. Before he could speak Simone ran towards the door and yelled, "Get out of my way!"

The servant moved and as Simone passed him he yelled at her, "Have you gone mad woman?!"

Simone completely ignored him as she ran after the rats.

The servant then thought that Simone had the plague and was in the latter stages of it, and so he went to the master's bedroom and knocked hard on the door since the master must have been deep asleep if he had not been woken up by Simone's ruckus.

The master woke up in a fright and yelled out, "What is the meaning of this?!" waking his wife up in the process.

He ran to the door and flung it open, yet before he could say anything the servant said, "Sir Farynor, the maid has gone mad, I think her to be with the plague and she has devastated the bakery."

"What?!" yelled the master, Thomas Farynor.

They both ran to the bakery, which was the kitchen, and saw that it was on fire in almost every spot that Simone had struck at the rats.

She had not noticed that almost everything was made out of wood.

Thomas and the servant ran in and began putting out the fires.

Simone meanwhile, killed the remaining two rats near the entry to the house.

Once Simone had composed herself she heard horses pulling a cart outside and a voice shouting, "Bring out your dead!" followed by the ring of a bell.

Curiosity got the better of her and so she opened the door. As she did, the driver of the cart saw Simone then stopped.

The bellman, who was also the one shouting, said to Simone, "Evening ma'am."

Both the driver and bellman tipped the brims of their hats to her, and the bellman continued, "Are you bringing out your dead?"

Simone remained calm and answered, "No dead here."

The bellman again tipped his brim and the driver drove off.

As the 'dead-cart' pulled away Simone looked at the back of it and saw dead bodies piled on top of each other. The rich and the poor together, there were no classes there. Some were clothed, some were naked.

In shock, she quickly turned away covering her nose and mouth with the apron she was wearing.

When the cart had departed, she looked out across to another house. A large red cross painted on the door caught her eye, "That's strange" she thought.

There was something written above the cross, also in red paint but Simone could not see what.

Once more curiosity got the better of her, she walked towards the house and when she got close enough she stopped and read aloud, "LORD HAVE MERCY ON US."

And then she glanced down at the handle of the door and noticed that it was locked from the outside with a chain and padlock.

Bewildered, she thought that the owners had locked up their house and left London.

All of a sudden, a man startled Simone as he yelled out,

"Oi! What you doin' there?" whilst frantically doing up the zipper of his pants.

The man did not get too close to her because he feared that she could be infected, and so he said to her, "Do not go near that house."

Simone asked, "Why not sir?"

The man replied, "Because the servant of that house had the plague and by law the house had to be shut up with everybody inside it, healthy or not, until everybody either perished, or by some miracle survived. Now the mother and her son are the only ones left alive, the rest of the family, including the servant, have been taken to the death-pits by cart. I am a watchman hired to watch over this dwelling to ensure nobody escapes."

Simone was shocked and replied to him in anger, "How can you do this? How can the government pass such a law? The people are prisoners in their own homes with death sentences."

The watchman replied, "I am just a poor man with a family of my own and no other means to support them. I do not take pleasure in this job, yet if I do not do this someone else will."

The watchman paused and then continued, "Personally, I think that this is God's vengeance for the crusades."

Simone was speechless at his last comment, and stared at him for a moment. She looked beyond him and saw other watchmen, she turned in the opposite direction and saw more of the same.

Then she looked back at the condemned house with tears in her eyes and with all of her strength she yelled out, "Kill every rat in your home and any flea you might find on yourself or on your children!"

She repeated that for a while until the servant of the Farynor house ran to the doorway and yelled at Simone, saying, "Stop yelling woman, and get back in here or else they'll lock us in aswell!"

Simone turned around and saw the servant running back inside, disappearing into a plume of smoke.

Simone wondered for a moment why there was smoke, and then she was filled with panic as she realised that she was the one who had caused it.

She ran to help, but when she entered into the house she froze! Simone backed up slowly outside and looked up at the sign above the entry to the house, the sign read 'Farynor Kings Bakery'.

Simone was stunned, her face became pale as she realised the severity of her actions and she yelled out, "What have I done?!"

She ran inside once more to try to help but it was too late.

Thomas Farynor, his wife, their daughter and their servant were trying to put out the fires throughout the bakery but to no avail.

Simone ran and grabbed a bed sheet from her room and swung it frantically trying to extinguish the fires.

Thomas yelled, "Everybody get out!"

His wife and daughter ran out crying.

Simone did not go but remained because of her guilt. Thomas grabbed her by the arm and said, "There is nothing you can do, let us go!"

Simone replied, "Let go of me, I am staying!" pulling her arm away.

The servant said to his master, "Sir, let us go, she will follow once the heat gets too much for her!"

Thomas nodded, and so they ran outside.

Simone became exhausted and gave up trying to put out the fire, her efforts were futile.

She ran to the nearest window, doing her best to avoid the flames along the way. She peered outside and saw the fire spreading rapidly to the adjoining buildings as most of the buildings were built of wood and thatch.

She cried even harder now and once more made a last desperate attempt to extinguish the flames.

Yet it was all in vain, the fire was all around her. She fell to her knees with tears running down her face, she looked up and said, "God, please forgive me."

She closed her eyes and said, "Return."

Simone was taken back home. She fell on the floor and wept, blaming herself for causing the Great Fire of London!

The fire lasted for four days and consumed what the plague could not touch.

It burnt more than half the city, destroying more than thirteen thousand homes.

The official death toll was 8 lives, these were people that were registered citizens of London. The number of poor people that perished was far greater.

All of a sudden, Simone stopped crying and sat up. She had had a revelation, and slightly relieved said aloud, "The fire killed off most of the rats and fleas."

She realised that it was a necessary loss to save the nation from the plague's imminent escalation.

The rebuilt London would be more spacious and never again be able to burn the way it did.

The plague never came back.

The revelation lifted her spirits slightly, even though the guilt of causing the fire was still very present.

She wanted to get her mind off of what had just happened and so she crawled over to the book and turned the page to reveal the next chapter..

Chapter Six
GENIUSES

A war raged in America in the late 1880s. A war of electrical currents.

Thomas Edison's Direct Current (DC) system powered the world.

Then came Nikola Tesla declaring that his Polyphase Alternating Current (AC) system was the future.

Before the 'war', Tesla was recommended to Edison and so he hired him. Edison offered Tesla a very large sum of money if he was able to redesign Edison's inefficient motors and generators.

Tesla did just that, but Edison broke his word and cheated Tesla out of his agreed money.

Tesla resigned.

George Westinghouse saw great potential in Tesla and so he hired him. Edison was very troubled, he knew that Tesla had secret ideas that were going to change the world, thus effecting Edison's inventions and in turn, his wealth.

Tesla declared that AC was much safer than DC and would also be infinitely more efficient. He also stated that AC did not need a substation every three kilometres to sustain the current, rather only one every hundreds of kilometres.

Edison saw that Tesla's Polyphase AC System was far superior to his DC System, thus began the 'war of currents'.

Edison tried to discredit AC with propaganda and smear campaigns.

Edison lobbied against Tesla's AC in state government, spreading false information on AC deaths and he also publicly killed animals to further discourage the use of AC.

In the end, due to public demand, the victor was Nikola Tesla, the man who was to electrify the world.

In 1893, the contract to harness Niagara Falls to generate electricity was awarded to Westinghouse due to Tesla's work.

Edison was furious.

The test was to transmit electricity and power the city of Buffalo thirty five kilometres away.

Tesla stated that using his AC system, Niagara Falls could power all of Eastern America, not just Buffalo alone.

Tesla designed and built the hydroelectric generators using his system. They successfully transmitted electrical power to Buffalo.

That same year at the World's Fair in Chicago, on a moonless night, at a poorly lit showground, thousands of people were gathered around the Grand Basin to see Tesla's AC system light up the fair.

Tesla stood on a platform with the fair officials and some politicians. He was given the go-ahead by the Mayor of Chicago.

Tesla nodded and walked up to the large lever on the edge of the platform. Wasting no time he pulled the lever down.

Success. The sight was magnificent, the multitudes were awestruck and everybody cheered.

That same night at the Fair a dinner party was held for all the dignitaries.

At the party, whilst the majority of the people present mingled on the main floor, Tesla was sitting by himself in his seat at the dinner table.

There were a small number of people seated around him at the other tables yet not at his.

Tesla was looking down at the table, yet staring at nothing. He was immersed in deep yet clear thought, his mind was elsewhere, he was concerned and agitated.

All of a sudden, he felt a person's hand on his right shoulder and that person spoke to him, "You are the man who lit up the world, and yet at this moment it looks like you are still living in darkness."

Tesla looked at the person. He smiled and greeted the visitor, "Albert Einstein" he said.

Immediately Simone found herself at the far side of the dining hall, at a window behind a curtain. She was disoriented, but quickly realised where she was and shuffled her way out from behind the curtain.

She then quickly made her way towards Tesla and Einstein. At the same time she noticed that she was wearing a long corseted dress, with a bustle and puffy sleeves, all of which she admired very much.

When Simone saw Tesla and Einstein she was excited and nervous. She saw a vacant chair at an empty table behind them and so she sat in it.

Wasting no time, she began to listen in on what Tesla and Einstein were saying, and just then a waiter approached her, and asked, "May I get you anything ma'am?"

"I am fine, thank you." answered Simone.

The waiter nodded and replied, "Ma'am" and walked away.

Simone continued to listen in.

Einstein was speaking, "..Before we go any further, I would like to say that it is an honour to meet you."

Tesla smiled, then replied, "Thank you Albert" then continued, "I've heard so much about you and I have also read most of your work, and some of it is very impressive."

"Thank you Tesla" Einstein replied, then continued, "Likewise, I too have read most of your work, and may I say that I found it electrifying."

Both of them laughed, and Einstein continued, "I very much admire the work that you have done and are still doing with electricity, and one day I would love to be a part of the magnificent electrical storm you produce and stand in the middle of, all the while remaining unscathed."

Tesla said, "You are welcome at any time Albert."

Einstein was very pleased with this.

Moving on, he then said, "Tesla, you are the most difficult man to keep up with. From my understanding, you have more than seven hundred patents and countless more unpatented inventions. What is also impressive is the fact that most of your inventions are extremely beneficial to mankind. From your Polyphase AC system to your wireless and cellular communication technology with radio. From controlling objects with a remote to your radar and laser technology. From your induction motor to your electrical generator. And let me not forget the hand-sized oscillator you invented that nearly brought down the whole building that your laboratory is in."

They both laughed. Tesla replied, "Yes, and with the same device I could have dropped the Brooklyn Bridge into the East River in less than an hour."

Both of them burst out laughing again.

Simone smiled and shook her head.

Einstein said to him, "Tesla, I believe that you are the most brilliant man alive, in fact I do not think there will ever come another who could overshadow you."

Tesla smiled and replied, "You are too kind Einstein, I thank you for your gracious words."

Simone was amazed at the fact that Tesla had accomplished so much for the world and yet she knew so little about him. She asked herself, "How can a man of unparalleled brilliance be neglected and forgotten?"

Einstein said to Tesla, "I am particularly fascinated with the 'fact' that you claim you can provide free wireless electrical energy to the entire planet. At first I thought it to be absurd, but then I reasoned that if an idea is not absurd, then there is no hope for it. Only those who attempt the absurd can achieve the impossible."

Einstein paused for a moment then continued, saying, "Tell me Tesla, is this truly possible?"

Tesla smiled and answered, "Yes it is, and that is a 'fact'."

Einstein was amazed and he said, "Fact?.. Tesla, that is astounding! That means every person on earth will have free energy, including the poor! You will, once again, change the world!"

Tesla smiled and replied, "Thank you once more for your kind words Einstein. I believe that is why I have been put on this earth, to change it, to harness its own forces for the service of mankind."

Tesla then said, "Now, about the free energy, when wireless is perfectly applied, the whole world will be converted into a huge brain. We shall be able to communicate with one another instantly, irrespective of distance. Not only this, but through television and telephony, we shall see and hear one another as perfectly as though we were face to face, despite intervening distances of thousands of kilometres; and the instruments through which we shall be able to do this will be amazingly simple compared to our present-day telephone. A person will be able to carry the device in their pockets. I have already designed the tower that will achieve all of this, yet I am concerned that the rich and powerful industrialists of the world will not stand for it, because most of them are set to lose their fortunes when energy is on the verge of becoming free for all, forever! I believe that they will pay off their governments to keep things as they are."

Simone shook her head in disgust. Einstein scoffed and said, "Great spirits have often encountered violent opposition from mediocre minds. The value of a person should be seen in what they give and not in what they are able to receive. The commonplace goals of human endeavour, possessions, outward success, luxury and publicity, to me these have always been contemptible. Each possession I own is a stone tied around my neck."

Tesla replied, "Einstein, I very much agree. Money does not represent such a value as men have placed on it. All of my money has been invested into experiments with which I have made new discoveries enabling mankind to have an easier life. The progressive development of man is vitally dependant on invention."

Einstein replied, "You are a humble and generous person, I respect that, keep doing what is right, it will gratify some and astonish the rest."

Tesla smiled humbly as Einstein continued, "Your imagination intrigues me, I believe it is more important than knowledge. For a true sign of intelligence is not knowledge, but rather, imagination. Logic will get you from A to Z, imagination will take you everywhere."

Tesla responded, "Well Einstein, my 'imagination' as you put it, *has* gotten me everywhere, although I must protest and replace 'imagination' with 'God', for it is He who has gotten me everywhere and has blessed me with my imagination. The gift of mental power comes from God, Divine Being, and if we concentrate our minds on that truth, we become in tune with this great power."

Einstein was bewildered by what Tesla had said, and replied, "How can a man of your calibre, of your stature believe in God?"

Simone shook her head and felt pity for Einstein.

Tesla answered, "How can I *not* believe in God when I see the evidence of creation all around me? Thus meaning that there *must* be a Divine Creator."

Einstein replied saying, "I understand that we are in the position of a little child entering a library filled with books written in many different languages, the child dimly suspects a mysterious order in the arrangement of the books but does not know what it is. We see a universe marvelously arranged and obeying certain laws, yet only dimly understand these laws. Our limited minds cannot grasp the mysterious force that moves the constellations. My sense of God is my sense of wonder for the universe. I do not believe in a God who rewards good and punishes evil."

Tesla looked at Einstein, bemused, and said to him, "Einstein, can you imagine a society where evil goes unpunished?"

Einstein replied, "I understand your point Tesla, yet my point is if people are good only because they fear punishment, and hope for reward, then those people are a sorry lot indeed."

Tesla said, "I see your point Einstein, a very good one indeed."

Einstein continued saying, "As a child I received instruction in the Bible and the Talmud. I am a Jew, but I am enthralled in the luminous figure of the Nazarene. No one can read the Gospels without feeling the actual presence of Jesus. His personality pulsates in every word. No 'myth' is filled with such life."

Simone found this offensive, but had to restrain herself from speaking.

Tesla frowned at Einstein and said to him, "Myth?.. What you are saying is very offensive, but in my qualities both as Christian and philosopher, I forgive you."

Simone smiled.

Einstein responded, "I do apologise Tesla, I sometimes get carried away, yet in my defense please let me say that truly Jesus is too colossal for the pen of phrasemongers, however artful. No man can dispose of Christianity with a witty remark."

Tesla replied saying, "I accept your apology Einstein, and I respect it, as scientists very rarely apologise."

They both laughed and Simone smiled.

Einstein said, "I am glad that we resolved that problem so quickly. A clever person solves a problem, a wise person avoids it. I must be a clever person."

They laughed again, then Einstein continued, "One must also say that significant problems we have, cannot be solved at the same level of thinking with which we created them.. For example, war."

Then Tesla replied, "O, how I loathe war. The word itself makes me shudder. I am to understand that you also have a healthy hatred for war?"

Einstein answered, "The very thought of it makes my blood run cold. Peace cannot be kept by force, it can only be achieved by understanding. We must be prepared to make the same heroic sacrifices for the cause of peace that we make ungrudgingly for the cause of war. The pioneers of a warless world are the people who refuse military service. It is my conviction that killing under the cloak of war, is nothing but an act of murder. And just as children do not heed the life experiences of their parents, in the same way nations ignore history. Bad lessons always have to be learnt anew. The world is a dangerous place, not because of those who do evil, but because of those of us who look on and do nothing."

Tesla smiled and said, "I am glad you said that Einstein, because I have decided to stop 'doing nothing'."

Einstein replied, "What do you mean Tesla?"

Tesla's expression became serious, he leant over to Einstein and said, "We both have great respect for one another and therefore trust one another. What I am about to tell you is classified as Top Secret from the government. Although, some of its secrets have been leaked to the media."

Tesla sighed then continued, "I have created 'the Super Weapon' that will put an end to all war. A charged particle beam projector the media is calling the 'Peace Ray', some even call it the 'Death Ray', I call it the 'Teleforce'."

Einstein became even more curious as Tesla continued, saying, "The Teleforce sends concentrated beams of particles through the air with such tremendous energy that they will cause armies to drop dead in their tracks. The voltage for propelling the beam to its objective will attain eighty million volts."

Einstein's eyes opened wide in disbelief as Tesla continued, "The tremendous speed of the electrical particles of matter will give them their destructive qualities and catapult them on their mission of defensive destruction. No possible defense could be devised against it, as the beam is all-penetrating."

Einstein, still shocked, asked, "That is a brilliant invention, but what if it falls into the wrong hands?"

Tesla answered, "Obviously, I have considered that as well, knowing full well that that might happen. I distributed portions of information about the Teleforce to the Russian, United Kingdom, Canadian and United States governments so that they would have to work together to piece the weapon together."

"Brilliant!" exclaimed Einstein, and he continued, "You have put those governments in mutual dependability. Tesla, I must say I am very thankful that you are on the side of good and not evil, for you would be able to bring the whole world down, having them beg for your mercy."

Tesla laughed and said, "Thank God?"

They paused, looking at one another and then burst out laughing and Simone smiled once more.

Then Tesla spoke, "But, there is more."

"More?" asked Einstein.

"Yes" answered Tesla, then continued, "I have built a flying machine."

Einstein, once more stunned by Tesla's statement replied, "Tesla, judging by your expression, you are not joking with me. This is almost unbelievable, this is marvelous."

Tesla replied, "I am not joking with you. The government is in possession of it, I proposed the plans and they asked me to build it. I gladly accepted, for it was one of my goals in life to build a flying machine."

Einstein asked, "Flying machine? How do you mean?"

Tesla replied, "If you were to see it on the ground you would never guess it could fly. Yet, it will be able to move at will through the air in any direction with perfect safety. It will be capable of immense speeds, regardless of the weather and it can remain absolutely stationary in the air hovering for a great length of time."

Tesla looked at the table they were sitting at and picked up an empty dish that was in front of him and turned it upside down placing it on top of the exact same dish that was in front of Einstein and said, "Look at these saucers, this is how my flying machine looks."

Simone, knowing that both of them were looking down at the table, turned around and saw what Tesla had presented to Einstein.

She turned back around and giggled because she knew what Tesla was talking about.

All of a sudden, she had a moment of realisation and said to herself, "They actually exist because of Tesla?"

She became even more amazed at him.

Einstein said, pointing at the saucers, "That is amazing, I can hardly wait to see one. Have you thought of what you might call your flying machine?"

Tesla answered, "No, I have not, it is referred to as the Tesla Flying Machine, although now that I displayed that example for you, I might call it the Flying Saucer."

They both laughed, Simone giggled quietly.

Tesla then said, "I think it would be wise of me to stop discussing my secret inventions any further."

"Wise decision" agreed Einstein and he continued, "Tesla, you have the world in your hands yet your appearance was one of concern when I approached you. Would it please you to ease your mind and talk to me about it?"

Tesla sighed and looked down at the table pausing for a moment, then said, "Einstein, I fear that Edison has plans to destroy me. I can understand his anger, yet he is not thinking of the benefits to mankind that my inventions have brought, and will continue to bring."

Einstein replied, "Tesla, anger dwells only in the bosom of fools."

"I agree" said Tesla, and he continued, "He has ordered his

men to follow me everywhere I go, I am positive that some of them are watching me right now."

At that very moment, a maitre d' approached Tesla and leant over saying, "Sir, I am afraid I have some unfortunate news."

Tesla and Einstein looked at one another as concern gripped their expressions.

The maitre d' continued, "I have just been informed that your laboratory has burned down."

Tesla, turned his head away and wept for a moment. But then he became furious and yelled, "My papers, my inventions.. my work! All gone!"

The people and the music fell silent as they all averted their attention to Tesla.

Simone looked down, closed her eyes and shook her head.

Tesla looked at Einstein and said to him, "It is of no coincidence that we were speaking of Edison immediately before I received this dreadful news."

Einstein placed his hand on Tesla's back and comforted him saying, "Now the world will truly know the type of man Edison is. Force always attracts men of low morality."

Simone did not want to be there anymore so she got up and made her way to the same place in which she had arrived, behind the curtain at the window.

She closed her eyes and said sadly, "Return", and she was taken back home.

When she arrived there, she took a moment to herself to reflect on all she had just witnessed. She truly realised how much easier a solitary man named Nikola Tesla had made her life.

With a great smile of appreciation on her face, she wasted no time in turning the page over to reveal the next chapter..

Chapter Seven
MOTHER

1930.. As soon as Simone read the year she was taken to a muddy sidewalk. It was a dark and rainy night.

Simone was lying on her back and the rain was hitting her face. She was on the verge of dying.

From her previous experiences with the book, she knew in her heart that she was there for a reason and that is why she did not 'return' herself back home at that moment.

In pain she cried out, groaning, the feeling was reminiscent of the time just before Jesus healed her.

Simone wept, and with a gentle voice, she once more pleaded, "God, help me."

All of a sudden, a young woman wearing a sari approached her. The woman smiled a peaceful smile and said to Simone, "I am here to help you."

Simone smiled back at her in gratitude, and extended her arms towards her.

The woman lifted her up and put Simone's arm around her, as Simone could not fully support herself.

The woman lived across the road from where Simone was.

"I will get you out of these wet and dirty clothes, then I will feed you and prepare a bed for you" the woman said.

"Thank you" whispered Simone.

Right then, Simone passed out.

What must have been hours later, she woke up in a bed, in a room lit by a small fire, and the woman who saved Simone was kneeling at her bedside, praying.

The woman saw that Simone had woken and she said to her, "Thank God you are alright."

Simone, still weak, smiled and replied, "Thank you for praying."

The woman smiled back and said, "We should always be praying, prayer is everyone's duty. People make up excuses, such as their busy lives are preventing them from praying. This cannot be. Also, prayer is not asking. Prayer is putting one's self in the hands of God, at His disposition, and listening to His voice in the depths of our hearts. One of my daily prayers is one of gratefulness, because God has helped me to continue what I am doing up until now. And another is to teach me how to pray better."

The woman smiled, then Simone asked, "You must know a lot about God?"

The woman smiled again and answered, "We know very little about God, but it is our duty to know as much as possible. Even when I help the poorest of the poor, the first thing most of them ask for is not bread or clothes, but God. Even though often they are dying of hunger and are naked. They ask me to teach them the word of God. People are hungry for God. Poverty has not been created by Him. We are the ones who have created poverty. When a poor person dies of hunger, it has not happened because God did not take care of them. It has happened because neither you nor I wanted to give that person what they needed. We have refused to be instruments of love in the hands of God to give the poor a piece of bread, to offer them clothes with which to ward off the cold. It has happened because we did not recognise Christ when, once more, He appeared under the guise of pain. We should not serve the poor like they *were* Jesus, we should serve the poor because they *are* Jesus."

The woman paused thoughtfully, then continued, "We treat the poor like they are a garbage bag in which we throw everything we have no use for. Such as, food that we do not like or that is going bad. Clothing that we do not want or would not wear goes into that 'garbage bag'. This does not show any respect for the dignity of the poor. In fact, the poor understand human dignity better. If they have a problem it is not lack of money, but the fact that their right to be treated humanely and with tenderness is not recognised. The poor do not need a condescending attitude, nor pity towards them. The poor need our love and our kindness. Only in heaven will we see how much we owe to the poor for helping us to love God better because of them. Keep the joy of loving God in your heart and share this joy with all."

The woman paused and Simone said to her, "Please tell me more."

The woman smiled and said, "I ask of you one thing, do

not tire of giving to the poor, but do not give your leftovers. Give until it hurts, until *you* feel the pain. Satisfy the poor's hunger by sharing with them whatever you have.. to share with them until you yourself feel what they feel. If you cannot feed a hundred people, then feed just one."

After a moment, she continued, "Open your heart to the love God instills in it. God loves you tenderly. What he gives to you is not to be kept under lock and key, but to be shared. The more you save, the less you will be able to give. The less you have, the more you will know how to share. I fear just one thing.. Greed. The love of money is what motivated Judas to sell Jesus. Let us humble ourselves and ask God, when it comes time to ask Him for something, to help us to be generous. Whoever is dependent on their money, or worries about it, is truly a poor person. If that person places their money at the service of others, then that person becomes rich, very rich indeed. We should not regard giving as an obligation, but as a desire."

The woman got up to tend to the fire, all the while still speaking to Simone, "There is also a different kind of poverty, in the form of abandonment and neglect. This is the most terrible poverty and it abides most in the developed countries. You have to ask yourself 'Do I know the poor in my own home?'. If there was more love, more unity, more peace, and more happiness within the family, there would not be so many alcoholics and drug addicts. Love is just like what Christ Himself showed with His death, the greatest gift. If we truly love one another we will not be able to avoid making sacrifices. If we really want to love, we must learn how to forgive. Unforgiveness is the poison people drink, all the while hoping the other person gets sick.

If we have no peace, it is because we have forgotten that we belong to one another. Jesus comes to meet us. To welcome Him, let us go to meet Him. He comes to us in the hungry, the naked, the lonely, the alcoholic, the drug addict, the prostitute, the street beggars. He may come to you in a father, in a mother, in a brother or in a sister who is alone. If we reject them, if we do not go out to meet them, we reject Jesus Himself. Also, do not judge them. Who are we to accuse anybody? Maybe *we* are the ones responsible for others doing things we think are not right. Let us not forget that we are dealing with our brothers and sisters. That leper, that sick person, that drunk, are *all* our brothers and sisters. They too, have been created by a greater Love. That is something we should never forget."

The woman stopped for a moment and reached for another blanket and laid it out over Simone. She began to speak again, "Life is a gift that God has given us. That life is present even in the unborn. A human hand should never end a life. I am convinced that the screams of the children whose lives have been terminated before their birth reach God's ears. The same principle applies to war, which is the killing of human beings. Who can even think that it could be 'just'? We must resist all evil and humble ourselves, for the path that will make us more like Jesus is humility. Holiness is not the luxury of a few. It is everybody's duty. A clean heart is a free heart. Purity, chastity, and virginity created a special beauty in Mary that attracted God's attention. He showed His great love for the world by giving Jesus to her. We all have the duty to serve God where we are called to do so. I feel that what I am doing is a drop in the ocean, but the ocean would be less because of that missing drop. As long as we make the best effort we are capable of, we cannot be discouraged by our failures. We cannot claim any success either. We should give God all of the credit and be extremely sincere when we do so."

Once the woman stopped speaking, Simone said to her, "You have truly touched and inspired me with your words. Now it is clear to me why God wanted me here."

They both smiled at each other. Then, Simone asked the woman, "May I know your name?"

The woman answered, "Oh, forgive me, I forgot to introduce myself when you woke. I would have before but you were sleeping. My name is Agnes."

Simone replied, "It has been wonderful listening to you Agnes, my name is Simone."

Agnes replied, "Thank you for listening to me Simone." They both giggled.

Simone tried to think of who Agnes could be, she appeared to be about twenty years of age at that moment in time. Simone was puzzled, and so she asked her, "Agnes, may I ask which city we are in?"

Agnes replied, "We are in Calcutta."

Simone's eyes opened wide and she started breathing heavily.

Agnes asked her, "Are you alright?"

Simone did not answer her question, but asked excitedly, "Agnes, where were you born?"

Agnes replied, "I was born in Macedonia's capital Skopje."

In her excitement Simone yelled out, "Mother Teresa!" startling Agnes in the process.

Agnes then asked, "Who is 'Mother Teresa'?"

"You are Mother Teresa!" answered Simone whilst laughing in amazement.

Agnes looked at Simone and said to her, "I think delirium is setting in."

Simone laughed and said to her, "No Agnes, I am in my right mind. But now I must leave. I thank you for rescuing me and taking care of me."

Agnes smiled and nodded her head, saying to Simone, "Do not forget your sari" whilst pointing to it hanging up on a hook. "I washed it while you slept" she continued.

Simone looked at the sari and was astounded.

It was the actual sari Simone had seen Mother Teresa wearing in pictures.

Simone climbed out of bed and said, "No" in amazement.

She looked at Agnes and then continued, "Please keep it as a gift from God."

Agnes smiled and replied, "That is very generous of you Simone, thank you."

Simone and Agnes embraced. Then Simone ran out of the room, out of the house and around the corner.

She stopped, leaning on the house, looked up into the starry night sky and said, "Thank You God for allowing me to see her."

Simone smiled to herself, closed her eyes and said, "Return."

She was taken back home.

Simone was so overwhelmed by the fact that she had just seen Mother Teresa.

She could not wait to find out what the next chapter might

have in store for her, so she turned the page over and revealed the next chapter..

Her excitement and happiness quickly changed when she read the title..

Chapter Eight

FÜHRER

1945.. Once more, as in the previous chapter, when Simone read the year she was taken to that time. She found herself in the empty room of a bunker.

As soon as she arrived she could hear gunfire and explosions outside. The earth trembled and the light in the room flickered.

Simone became frightened and said aloud, "God, where am I?"

Then she remembered the title of the chapter and was alarmed. With a quiet voice she whispered, "Hitler.."

Then she continued, pleading, "God, why did you bring me here to this evil place?"

She then realised that she was there for a reason, as in the previous chapter, so again trusting in God, she did not 'return' herself back home at that very moment.

Confused, she did not know what to do. She sat down in a chair and stared at the door of the room.

She could hear the busy sounds of the people inside the bunker.

Simone walked up to the door then put her hand on the handle and paused for a moment, gathering her thoughts.

She then opened the door slowly and saw members of the SS and the Gestapo running around.

She quickly closed the door and leant back against it exclaiming, "I can't do this!"

She closed her eyes and paused there for a moment. Then she opened her eyes and proclaimed, "I must do this."

So, she opened the door, and standing there was Joseph Goebbles, Simone recognised him from pictures she had seen of him.

Her eyes filled with tears because she knew that he was responsible for the deaths of millions of people.

Goebbles said to Simone, "He wants to see you." And then he left.

She closed the door and became nauseated.

After a moment, anger settled in, she wiped the tears from her eyes and opened the door for the third time and walked out of the room.

She walked about, amongst everyone for a short while and then an SS officer noticed that she looked very disorientated.

He walked over to her and said, "Follow me!"

Simone became very nervous as the officer led her to a door and said, "He is waiting for you."

Simone looked at him and paused.

"Thank you" she stuttered, realising she had to give an answer. She opened the door, walking in backwards as she closed it between them.

She did not turn around immediately because she was not ready to see who she thought she was going to see.

She thought to herself, "How does anyone prepare themselves to meet *him*?"

She began breathing heavily as she stared at the door, then she heard his voice saying, "Ah Eva, there you are."

Simone's eyes opened wide and she became even more nauseated than before as she realised who she was; Eva Braun, Hitler's wife.

"Come here Eva" said Hitler.

Simone took a deep breath and slowly turned around.

When she saw him she instantly began to cry.

"What's wrong Eva?" said Hitler, as he walked over to her and put his arms around her.

Simone screamed and jumped out of his grasp.

"Eva.. Calm down my darling. It is I." he said.

Simone cried even more now.

Then she spotted a Luger pistol on Hitler's desk, so she ran to it, snatched it up and pointed it straight at Hitler's head.

Hitler was shocked, "Eva, what are you doing?!" he asked.

Simone replied, "Stop it! Stop calling me that name!"

She caught her breath then continued angrily, "Now it is time for you to pay for what you have done!"

Hitler replied, "Eva, you've gone mad!"

Her hands shook as she squeezed at the trigger.

But right at that moment, she heard Jesus speak to her once more, saying, "There is no mercy in him, he has been given many chances through life to repent, yet there is neither mercy nor forgiveness in him. Therefore, My Father will not forgive him. Yet Simone, you *must* forgive Him.. for *your* sake. Do not carry the burden of unforgiveness the rest of your life. For God said, 'Vengeance is mine, I will repay'."

Simone clenched her teeth and grasped the pistol even tighter.

A moment passed.

Then Simone began to weep. She closed her eyes, bowed her head and said, "Lord, I forgive him."

She loosened her grip on the pistol and was about to put it down when all of a sudden, Hitler leapt towards Simone in an attempt to disarm her, but as he grabbed at the pistol she panicked and pulled on the trigger.

The bullet went straight through Hitler's heart.

Simone was shocked and dropped the pistol.

Hitler grabbed hold of Simone to support himself, but he fell to his knees, holding her arms and said to her, "Eva.. why?"

Simone was speechless.

He dropped at her feet, dead.

Hitler had died at the hands of a Jew.

The sound of the pistol discharging echoed through the bunker and so the SS and Gestapo stormed the room. They could not believe their eyes, their Führer was dead.

Goebbles made his way through the men and froze when he saw Hitler on the floor.

He then looked at the Luger, and then at Simone.

Simone looked at Goebbles and said to him, "My name is Simone and I am a Jew."

Goebbles was enraged and screamed, "Kill her!!"

Everything seemed to move in slow motion and right before the men fired at her, Simone smiled at Goebbles, closed her eyes and said, "Return."

As she was being taken back to her apartment she heard the machine gun fire fade away behind her, as Eva Braun was being executed.

When she arrived back home she felt immense relief. A great burden had been lifted off of her as despite the final outcome, she had found the strength to forgive.

THE FINAL CHAPTER

Simone gazed out of the window next to her and noticed that the sun had risen.

She looked down at the book on the table and saw that she had come to the end.

"What an abrupt ending" she thought to herself.

She realised that even though she had not slept, she had no desire to as her excitement would not subside.

She sat down by the window, staring out of it and thought of the night's unbelievable events with a smile of amazement on her face.

Suddenly, her thoughts were interrupted by the high pitched sound of an airplane.

"That's strange" she said.

Then her apartment began to shake as the large airplane flew overhead and appeared through her window.

That scared Simone and she jumped back, bumping into the table on which she had placed the book.

The force knocked the book onto the floor.

Simone stood up and rushed back to the window. While she was looking at the airplane she was puzzled, "Why is that airplane flying so low?" she thought.

But then her attention was averted to the book which was producing a tearing sound.

It was on the floor, opened at its back cover.

The sound was a page tearing off of the back cover, separating from it.

Simone was stunned.

She looked on in curiosity as the book birthed a new chapter.

Then, numbers began to appear in print at the top of the page.. 9/11.

Simone was confused and questioned, "What is 9/11?"

She looked back outside the window in contemplation and at that very moment saw the same large airplane crash into one of the towers of the World Trade Centre, exploding into flames.

Simone screamed and began to cry. She could hardly believe her eyes.

In a flurry, more new pages were being created from the back cover of the book, as history was again being written.

THE END..?

Afterword & Conclusion:

Imagine His Story

*L*et us, for a moment, truly imagine Jesus' story.

Most people understand that Jesus was a man who lived in Israel about 2000 years ago. Most religions in the world view Jesus as a Prophet and/or a good teacher. Yet whilst those things are true, they do not capture who He truly is.

Jesus is the Son of God, God made into flesh!

Jesus Christ existed from the beginning with God and the Holy Spirit. He was sent to earth by God to die for our sins and in that way He paid the penalty of our sins so that we would not be separated from God for an eternity in constant torment in hell.

As God, Jesus' death provided forgiveness for the sins of the entire world. Because mankind's sin has been paid for by our sinless Saviour, God who is Holy can now forgive our sins when we accept Jesus' payment as our own.

Jesus Christ's love is shown in His leaving His heavenly throne, coming to earth as a man where He would be mocked, betrayed, beaten and crucified on a cross, rising from the dead on the third day as He said He would.

The bodily resurrection of Jesus proves that God accepted

His death as the payment for our sins. When Jesus rose from the dead He proved His victory over sin, death, and hell.

The resurrection is the most important event in history providing evidence that Jesus is who He claimed to be - the Son of God.

It validated the many prophecies in the Old Testament of the Bible declaring His coming, birth, life, death, and resurrection. It validated the message of love and forgiveness through His sacrifice, even though it cost Him everything and even though we are unworthy of such love.

The message of the cross is that you are worth dying for.

In the person of Jesus Christ, God sacrificed Himself on our behalf. Jesus took the punishment that we deserve in order to save us from an eternity in hell.

You may ask why it matters whether Jesus is God or not? The answer is both clear and simple: If Jesus is not God, then His death would not have achieved our eternal redemption, something only God could do. He had to come in the form of a man so that He could die. But as He is also God, death and hell could not hold Him and He defeated both with His resurrection thereby purchasing our salvation by the shedding of His blood. Salvation is a gift from God, only available through faith in Jesus Christ.

Jesus' deity is why He proclaimed, "I am the way and the truth and the life. No one comes to the Father except through Me."

We have all fallen short of the glory of God because of sin, thus we are separated from Him. Jesus didn't just come to deliver us from our 'sins', the act of sin, He came to deliver us from our 'sin', the state of sin.

You were born into the state of sin before you committed an act of sin. You inherited it.

If we say that we have no sin, we deceive ourselves, and the truth is not in us. If we say that we have not sinned, we make God a liar.

The fact that God hates sin means that He hates being separated from us. God's hatred of sin implies that He loves us and wants to bless us.

Sin lures us to focus on the pleasures of the world thus denying us access to God's blessings.

Do not love the world or the things in it. The world is under the control of the devil. What will profit a man if he gains the whole world and loses his own soul?

Whoever commits sin is a slave of sin.

So how can we be set free from slavery, from the 'state' of sin, from the separation from God?

The only answer is through God's only Son, Jesus Christ our Lord and Saviour! Through His shed blood!

We have been cleansed by His blood, redeemed by His blood, forgiven by His blood, justified by His blood, sanctified by His blood, reconciled to God by His blood! We have victory over the devil through His blood! We have eternal life through His blood!

Only by believing in Jesus through His shed blood do we have a right to know God, to enter into His presence before His throne, a right to enter Heaven, a right to everlasting life.

It is not achieved by being a good person or doing good works, although these are admirable traits. It is ONLY through Jesus Christ the Messiah! Who was slain, and has redeemed us to God by His blood: out of every tribe, and tongue, and people and nation.

Jesus' death on the cross was His purpose for coming to earth. To die as God's eternal sacrifice for all mankind (that includes YOU!). He died to save us from wrath and an eternal separation from God and Himself.

Just before He died on the cross, Jesus said, "It is finished" declaring that the work of eternal redemption was once and for all completed.

We have not been redeemed with corruptible things, but with the precious blood of the Messiah.

It was your sin and my sin that crucified Him. In that way, God demonstrated His love towards us, in that while we were still sinners, Christ died for us.

In conclusion, where will you spend eternity? With God in Heaven or without Him in hell?

It is your choice!

If you want to spend eternity with God the gift of salvation is simple.

First, you must realise you are a SINNER. The punishment of you being a sinner is death, but after that you will be judged.

So before you die you must REPENT of your sins, it is God's command. If you do not repent you will perish. God's will is that none should perish but rather all come to repentance.

But, realising that you are a sinner and repenting does NOT save you! So what does?

You must believe in the Lord Jesus Christ and you will be saved! Call upon His name and *be* saved! Just believe in Him as the one who bore your sin, died in your place and whom God raised from the dead. It is that simple!

His resurrection ensures you will claim eternal life when you receive Jesus as your Lord and Saviour.

How do we receive Him?

Just pray out loud:

God, I know that I am a sinner and I know that because of my sin I deserve to be eternally separated from You. I am sorry for all of my sins. I believe that Jesus is Your Son and that He was my substitute when He died on the Cross. I believe His shed blood, death, and resurrection were for me. I now receive Him as my Lord and Saviour. I thank You for loving me, thank You for providing the Sacrifice, thank You for the forgiveness of my sins, the gift of salvation and eternal life, because of Your merciful grace. Lord Jesus Christ, I ask that You come into my life right now. Amen.

If you truly meant what you just prayed and received it by faith you have been set free and have passed from death to life. You have turned your life over to God and have become His child, a new creation.

When a person receives salvation and becomes 'born again', God's word declares that their sins are not remembered against them. It is as if they were never committed!

Jesus said, "Unless you are born again you can not see the Kingdom of God."

The moment you become born again the Holy Spirit will live within you. He is the One who revealed Jesus to you in the first place. Through His power we are able to resist and overcome sin because sin grieves Him.

Confess what God has done for you, live for Him, praise and worship Him, get baptised, partake in communion, pray, read the Bible, and tell others about Jesus! For He said, "Therefore whoever confesses Me before people, them I will also confess before My Father (God), Who is in Heaven."

The world must know that Jesus is ALIVE!

You have been forgiven because of God's love, mercy and grace. He loves mankind so much that He still created us knowing the heartache it would cause Him to redeem us.

Yet the love which Jesus shows towards us on the Cross is not all, when we place our faith in Him, as our personal Lord and Saviour, He comes to dwell within us through the Holy Spirit.

Imagine His Prophecy

*H*ere are just a few prophecies written about Jesus many centuries before His birth!

These first six verses listed here from the Book of Psalms refer to the scene of Jesus' suffering on the Cross. The verses following these are explained individually:

Psalm 22:1

My God, My God, why have You forsaken Me?

Psalm 22:15

My strength is dried up like a potsherd, and My tongue clings to My jaws; You have brought Me to the dust of death. For dogs have surrounded Me;
16

The congregation of the wicked has enclosed Me. They pierced My hand and My feet.
18

They divide My garments among them, and for My clothing they cast lots.

Psalm 31:5

Into Your hands I commit My spirit.

Psalm 34:20

He guards all His bones; not one of them is broken.

Psalm 41:9

Even My own familiar friend in whom I trusted, who ate My bread, has lifted up his heel against Me.

(The person spoken of here was Judas Iscariot)

Psalm 69:4

Those who hate Me without a cause are more than the hairs of My head; being My enemies wrongfully, though I have stolen nothing, I still must restore it.

Psalm 69:9

Zeal for Your house has eaten Me up, and the reproaches of those who reproach You have fallen on Me.

(This refers to when Jesus drove away the swindling merchants from the Temple).

Psalm 78:2

I will open My mouth in a parable.

(Jesus spoke in parables many times).

Psalm 118:22

The stone which the builders rejected has become the chief cornerstone.

26

Blessed is He who comes in the name of the Lord.

From the Book of Isaiah:

Isaiah 7:14

Therefore the Lord Himself will give you a sign: Behold, the virgin shall conceive and bear a Son, and shall call His name Immanuel. (Which means 'God with us').

(This refers to Mary birthing Jesus Christ).

Isaiah 9:6

For unto us a child is born, unto us a Son is given; and the government will be upon His shoulder. And His name will be called Wonderful, Counselor, Mighty God, Everlasting Father, Prince of Peace.

Isaiah 49:6

I (God) will also give You (Jesus) as a light to the Gentiles (non-Jews), that You should be My salvation to the ends of the earth.

Isaiah 53:3-9

He is despised and rejected by men, a Man of sorrows and acquainted with grief. And we hid, as it were, our faces from Him; He was despised, and we did not esteem Him.

Surely He has borne our griefs and carried our sorrows; yet we esteemed Him stricken, smitten by God, and afflicted.

But He was wounded for our transgressions, He was bruised for our iniquities; the chastisement for our peace was upon Him, and by His stripes we are healed.

All we like sheep have gone astray; we have turned, everyone, to his own way; and the Lord has laid on Him the iniquity of us all.

He was oppressed and He was afflicted, yet He opened not His mouth; He was led as a lamb to the slaughter, and as a sheep before its shearers is silent, so He opened not His mouth.

He was taken from prison and from judgment. For He was cut off from the land of the living; for the transgressions of My people He was stricken.

And they made His grave with the wicked.

Isaiah 53:11-12

He shall see the labour of His soul, and be satisfied. By His knowledge My righteous Servant shall justify many, for He shall bear their iniquities.

Therefore I will divide Him a portion with the great, and He shall divide the spoil with the strong, because He poured out His soul unto death, and He was numbered with the transgressors, and He bore the sin of many, and made intercession for the transgressors.

FROM THE BOOK OF JEREMIAH:

Jeremiah 7:11

Has this house, which is called by My name, become a den of thieves in your eyes.

(Again, this is referring to Jesus driving out the merchants from the Temple).

Jeremiah 31:15

Thus says the Lord: a voice was heard in Ramah, lamentation and bitter weeping, Rachel weeping for her children, refusing to be comforted for her children, because they are no more.

(King Herod ordering the killing of all male children who were in

those districts from 2 years old and under, hoping to kill the Messiah, the baby Jesus).

FROM THE BOOK OF HOSEA:

Hosea 11:1

Out of Egypt I called My Son.

(Joseph, Mary and Jesus stayed in Egypt until King Herod died. God then told Joseph, through an angel, to return Jesus to Israel).

FROM THE BOOK OF MICAH:

Micah 5:2

But you, Bethlehem Ephrathah, though you are little among the thousands of Judah, yet out of you shall come forth to Me the One to be Ruler in Israel, whose goings forth are from of old, from everlasting.

FROM THE BOOK OF ZECHARIAH:

Zechariah 9:9

Rejoice greatly, O daughter of Zion! Shout, O daughter of Jerusalem! Behold, your King is coming to you; He is just and having salvation, lowly and rising on a donkey, a colt, the foal of a donkey.

(Speaks of Jesus' triumphal entry into Jerusalem on Palm Sunday on a colt).

Zechariah 12:10

And I will pour on the house of David and on the inhabitants of Jerusalem the Spirit of grace and supplication; then they will look to Me whom thy pierced. Yes, they will mourn for Him as one mourns for his only son, and grieves for him as one grieves for a firstborn.

Zechariah 13:7
Strike the Shepherd, and the sheep will be scattered.
(Jesus stricken and His Apostles scattering).

FROM THE BOOK OF MALACHI:

Malachi 3:1
"Behold, I send My messenger, and He will prepare the way before Me. And the Lord, whom you seek, will suddenly come to His temple, even the Messenger of the covenant, in whom you delight. Behold, He is coming!" says the Lord of hosts.
(The first messenger spoken of here is John the Baptist. The second Messenger is Jesus.)

FOR THE JEWS

*W*hy have Jews and Gentiles grown apart?

God never intended to start a *new* religion. It's not Judaism and Christianity, two streams of God, but the convergence of Jew and Gentile into ONE stream called the "One New Man".

God wants to gather together in *one* all things in Christ (Messiah). For He Himself is our peace, who has made both (Jew and Gentile) *one,* and has broken down the middle wall of separation to create in Himself One New Man in whom you also are being built together for a dwelling place of God in the Spirit.

The tabernacle prophesied by Amos is a type of the One New Man glorious congregation.

On that day God will raise up the tabernacle of David (the Jewish people), which has fallen down, and repair it's damages; He will raise up its ruins, and rebuild it as in the days of old; that they may possess the remnant of Edom (Septuagint reads 'mankind'), and all the Gentiles who are called by God's name.

The tabernacle of David was a unique temple. There was no separation between the people and God. There was no 'Holy of Holies'. Everybody experienced God's presence.

God promised that once the tabernacle of David was restored, it would cause a revival among the Gentiles. This was the proof text to convince the Apostles at the Jerusalem Council meeting to evangelise the Gentiles.

After Yeshua died, the veil of the temple was torn in two.

Now nothing should separate us from God. Yet, the middle wall of separation between Jews and Gentiles hinders the church from achieving its full destiny in God because the majority of Jewish people are excluded.

The Old Covenant glory is the "former rain". When the former rain joins with the "latter rain", or the New Covenant glory, there will be a move of God like the world has never seen. In other words, the Jew needs the Gentile Christian and the Gentile Christian needs the Jew for a full release of God's glory from the tabernacle of David. The One New Man is the reformation that will cause the restoration of intimacy with God that was experienced in the tabernacle of David and in the early church.

MESSIAH BEN JOSEPH AND MESSIAH BEN DAVID:

If you have diligently studied these prophecies, you would have realised that Yeshua (Jesus Christ) is both Messiah Ben Joseph and Messiah Ben David.

It is not two Messiahs making one appearance; it is rather one Messiah making two different appearances!

HEBREWS:

My Jewish brothers and sisters, read the book that was written for you.

Hebrews, in the New Testament, of the Holy Bible.

The New Testament is concealed in the Old Testament and the Old Testament is revealed in the New Testament.

The law was given through Moses, but grace and truth came through Yeshua.

ABOUT THE AUTHOR

Pero Kovaceski was born in the town of Ohrid, Macedonia.

From a young age he developed a passion for writing. This love which is still very much present to this day is clearly evidenced here in his first published novel, Imagine History.

He and his family migrated to Sydney, Australia, where Pero spent most of his early years.

It is where he now lives with his wife, Bronwyn, but they enjoy visiting Macedonia regularly.

BIBLIOGRAPHY

- Scripture taken from the New King James Version. Copyright © 1979, 1980, 1982 by Thomas Nelson, Inc. Used by permission. All rights reserved. Emphasis added.

- One New Man Interview – Sid Roth. From the 'Sid Roth's It's Supernatural & Messianic Vision' website. http://www.sidroth.org/site/PageServer?pagename=abt_faq_onenewman Accessed 15th November 2012.

- GotQuestions?org website. http://www.gotquestions.org/ Accessed multiple times between 9th September – 15th November 2012.